N G SANDERS
TO DIE FOR

AND THEN THERE WERE MORE

A TRILOGY OF STAND-ALONE NOVELS

Copyright © 2020 N G Sanders

These stories are works of fiction. Names, characters, places, and incidents are either products of the author's imagination or used fictitiously. Any resemblance to actual events, locales, or persons, living or dead, is entirely coincidental.

All rights reserved.

No part of this publication can be reproduced or transmitted in any form or by any means, electronic or mechanical, without permission in writing from N G Sanders.

Front Cover by Warren Design

Printed by CreateSpace and Amazon KDP
Printed in the United States of America
Available from Amazon.com and other retail outlets

First Printing Edition, 2020

For my wife, and partner in crime, Sam

To Die For

Anna's Xmas Dinner Party Guest List

Patrick
Careful what you say to him, Patrick's a shrink!

Grace
Being a GP, she's qualified to prescribe us with the fastest cure for a hangover!

Jack
After our indulgence, PT Jack will whip us back into shape for the New Year!

Jeff
Always up for a good time, no matter where or when. I warn you all, Jeff still parties like a rock star from the nineties!

Dennis
The only guy I know who makes a living from scribbling down his own thoughts on life!

Simon
A man of many talents. Certain to be in a different line of business from when we last met. I'll wager a magnum of champagne on it!

Tony
Always knows where best to invest your money so that you can waste even more of it – on say extravagant gatherings such as this!

Terry

Always macho, always moody. Make sure he has a drink in his hand when he arrives, please.

Ronnie

The wild teenage Ronnie I used to know and love led a bad example for all to follow. Can the headmaster still do it?

(This guest list was later recovered by forensics from Anna's home)

"Somehow our devils are never quite what we expect when we meet them face to face."

Nelson Demille

PART 1

Journeys end in lovers meeting

Chapter One

I

Ronnie

The owner of the hunting store stood an impressive six-foot-six and two-hundred-and-fifty pounds of Yankee named Bob. Outside Bob's store, two larger flagpoles either side of the Austrian flag were flying high with stars and stripes for all to see.

"You're right. Anyone can register for a permit, but it takes time," Bob gestured to the wall of rifles around him, gleaming behind polished reinforced glass. "We don't just hand these out to anyone. Not anymore."

Ronnie removed ten crisp five-hundred-Euro notes from his leather wallet, counting as he placed them on the counter.

"What're you doing?" Bob asked, but the look in his eye told Ronnie he knew exactly what he was doing.

Bob's brows converged in anger.

"I can get more."

"It's not a question of more," Bob replied, scratching his stubble. "I mean, buddy you look okay to me. But..." Bob removed his hunter's cap, scratching his receding hairline. "No can do," he finished decisively, still not wanting to look at the cash.

"That's not how we do business around here, understand?"

"Well, thanks for nothing much at all, I guess," Ronnie said, scooping up his five-thousand-Euros from the counter and turning to leave.

"Hey?"

"What?" Ronnie said with hope as he turned around, but could see right away from Bob's set face that this wasn't a change of heart.

"Do yourself a favour and wait for the permit," Bob said. "Don't try and get one on the black market, because you won't. At least not one that will fire. And flashing your cash around like that to the wrong guy, you'll either get beaten up or killed."

"Sure," Ronnie said. "I'll be back in a couple of weeks."

"I'll do you a special discount."

Ronnie wasn't going to sit around and just wait for this nutter to come and get him. It felt safer being on the move. But he couldn't very well spend the rest of his life looking over his shoulder and worrying about Anna. Angela, he'd meant his wife Angela. A twinge of guilt hit him then.

No, this trip was not just about Anna, although to refuse to recognise that he still did care for her would be yet another delusion he could not escape.

His neck ached from falling asleep on the train. He'd taken the Eurostar which had stopped at Cologne and Brussels. He'd booked a couchette, but had upgraded to a two-berth sleeper in consideration of his back and yet he still felt like he'd emerged post-op.

The journey from Vienna to Innsbruck had proven a more pleasant experience due to the spectacularly uplifting scenery. It was everything the brochure had promised.

Once in Innsbruck, Ronnie searched for somewhere to eat, heavily weighed down by a rucksack on his back and a suitcase with wheels that wouldn't roll freely and easily as it was designed to, making him jerk in half circles every ten yards or so. He also felt weighed down by the suddenly overcast weather and the rumours of a potential snowstorm related to him by the tourist information woman.

"Very bad Friday," she warned, pronouncing 'bad' as 'bat'. "Very bad. Worst in fifty years, they're telling me."

"You're kidding, I just got here."

"No one will be able to get out of their homes for days if they're right." She pointed to the queues across the road. "Supermarkets are already selling out."

A young girl who reminded him of Anna caught his eye as she passed by snapping pictures with a digital Go Pro camera. He'd been in this part of the country with Anna less than a decade ago. It seemed fantastic, another lifetime, and in a sense it was. He was a different man these days, his impulsiveness had gone with middle-age and his certain love for Angela cut through his defences.

Shouldn't have come. Ronnie's rational voice in his head scolded him. *No way on earth I should have made this trip.*

Ronnie had been hurt for a while, but then Angela had come along and taken all that hurt away as only Angela could with a thousand acts of kindness. The need for an exciting travelling existence had evaporated with their tender bond of equal partnership – along with the rebel forays of a misspent youth. He was twenty-something pounds heavier, hair-line receding and didn't care how Anna might perceive that if she even recognised him. And that was due to Angela and the comforting love she'd provided them with.

But the mystery of Anna had remained and why she had taken off so suddenly. He'd considered, being an academic man at heart, to write his memoirs of the whole episode but his love of teaching and later tutoring from home in his free time had meant he'd not found the time to do so.

He had attempted it one rainy Sunday afternoon but quickly found himself to be a man of science only, not of English, not of the arts.

There was so much in life he'd left undone, and this more than anything was fulfilling a need. The only need Angela could not satisfy perhaps.

A need to end a chapter that part of him felt guilty for even beginning. A chapter of his life he had to grit his teeth to face again. A chapter threatening to bring about a whole new him once again. And that was the magic, the wonder and the danger Anna brought with her.

His worst fear was that Anna had been taken against her will by this psychopath all those years ago and had derailed both their fates into something it shouldn't have been. That was why he was here, albeit against his own better judgment. Ronnie once again felt the unease of reacquainting himself with a past love.

Ronnie hailed a taxi, still thinking of Anna when he arrived at his guesthouse in Igls.

II

Jack

The whisky burned, but Jack needed it. He took another slug as cars whooshed by in the darkness.

"Want a sip?"

The taxi driver, his eyes dark and bloodshot, gave Jack a disapproving look in the rear-view mirror.

"Guess not."

Jack smiled as he tucked the duty-free booze away in his Adidas sports bag beside him on the backseat. The sports bag his only luggage, a bag that would have constituted hand luggage for most.

Jack made an effort to keep up with the driver's disjointed monologue. His driver's ID dangled from the front windscreen, the surname unpronounceable, with more letters in it than Schwarzenegger.

The driver, to Jack's amazement, turned the overhead light on to text on the deserted road and it was Jack's turn to sport a disapproving look.

"Do you mind?" Jack said.

"What?"

"Forget it," Jack said. "Doesn't matter."

It didn't pay to piss people off when you were miles from anywhere. Especially a temperamental savage-looking cabbie who could drop him off at the roadside in a second.

Jack fidgeted with his Nike baseball cap before deciding on reversing it. He felt cold despite his Ralph Lauren fleece sweater and a tight Lycra undershirt that hugged every contour of his toned physique.

He'd felt nauseated since the flight by the smell of the airline meal he hadn't realised he'd paid for on-line. He was just as nauseated by the sight of the Europabrucke. The driver had soberly informed him that the Europabrucke (suddenly taking on the role of tour guide presumably in the hope of a more substantial tip) was the highest road bridge in Europe.

No kidding, Jack thought. *Just keep your eyes on the road then, so as we don't end up going off it.*

The cabbie's one-handed texting over, Jack didn't appreciate the way the cabbie switched lanes without checking his blind spot. Mirrors remained largely unused aside from the disapproving looks he exchanged with a now severely pissed off Jack in the rear-view mirror. Jack had spent six months as a driving instructor before enrolling himself in college and getting his qualifications as a personal trainer. Jack hated sloppy people in both fields.

"Not like home, no?"

"Yeah, it's a lot different from home," Jack said, answering the cabbie's question while glancing out the window. "A lot different."

"Home's not as pretty as Austria, I'm thinking."

"Not as pretty," Jack replied dutifully.

What was he doing here, going God knows where? He was low on funds as it was. Why hadn't he just deleted the texts and e-mails before he'd read them? That would have been the sensible thing to do. The sane thing to do.

That answer was easy. Anna.

Anna was like no other woman he'd dated nor met since. If there was a chance that Anna could be back in his life, he felt he could do great things. And he liked the thought of that. The comfort of a regular girlfriend he wanted as much as she desired him.

A girlfriend who wasn't with you only because of the fear of facing life alone or another single mother interviewing for a vacant daddy spot.

The thought of settling down with Anna held no fear and that seemed amazing to him.

"You're here for a woman, no?" the driver said, meeting Jack's eyes in the mirror. "I can tell."

"How?" Jack replied flatly.

"The edginess."

"Oh."

"A woman not your wife, I'm thinking."

Jesus. Jack thought. *Trust me to get the only psychic cabbie in Europe.*

Jack rubbed his stubble and met the cabbie's stare in the rear-view mirror again.

"Yeah, a woman," Jack replied, looking distractedly out of the window. "You married?"

The cabbie laughed a raspy chuckle like the transmission of an old banger starting up. "Me? Married?" The laugh wheezed again. "No."

"Smart man."

The driver's moustache was twitching which meant he was playing tour guide again. Jack feigned politeness.

"How much further is it?"

Had he replied six miles or six minutes? Jack wasn't sure which because of the thickness of the accent he'd spoken in. Jack guessed six minutes because they measured all their distances in kilometres out here, the speedometer and road signs oblivious to miles.

Minutes later, the driver thanked Jack for his five-euro tip and wished him luck with his woman as he sped off into the night, texting whoever it was he was texting.

It was no surprise to Jack that his 'hotel' was little more than a glorified wooden shack that could only be said to be warm.

His room was at the end of the corridor. There seemed barely a dozen rooms in this hotel.

He lit a cigarette, his first of the day. Jack hadn't been able to light up in the taxi, again through fear that the unreadable driver would just dump him. Jack had noted the Bible on the front seat and the St. Christopher's statue on the dashboard. Everybody out here seemed religious.

It was inescapable. Even the decor of the room Jack was sat in thinking about this was religiously themed. There was a large picture of a blazing Christ with a glowing head above the bed that freaked him out a little. Jack had experimented with arson briefly as a kid. It had given him a thrill. A thrill soon surpassed by the pursuit of women.

Feeling lonely, Jack took another sip of the whisky between long indulgent drags of his cigarette. He ordinarily only drank in the company of women in clubs on Saturday nights and was down to five-a-day on his smokes. This was due to the combination of a poor VO2 Max score on his last testing serving as a wake-up call and the Paul McKenna *I Can Make You Quit Smoking* hypnosis audiobook he didn't leave home without, doubled up with a copious supply of Wrigley's spearmint gum and Nicorette.

The McKenna audiobook was a Christmas present from a girl he couldn't even recall. Nor the girl who'd given him the iPod for his birthday to play it on.

His only gift to them, himself. God's gift, they'd all joked.

And that just about summed it up for him. That was his life. Thirty-two now but looking twenty-five tops, and that was what counted. Beyond that, he was lost in every way that mattered. That was the reason he was out here in the middle of nowhere. Out here clinging to the past.

Beneath the healthy, friendly facade of neatly proportioned tanned aquiline features, beneath the gentle but piercing eyes like chips of sky, beneath the boy band dimples girls frequently surmised as "cute", he was a loser.

There was no other word for it. Good looks disguised a multitude of sins and incompetent acts, for which Jack was sincerely grateful. But Jack was ever mindful that it could only do so for so long. His lifestyle wouldn't look so attractive at forty, and wouldn't accommodate him at fifty. Perhaps even make him a laughing stock.

He looked around the very basic room with an appraising eye. "What a shithole."

Jack vowed that this would be the last time he'd have to settle for a room like this. Austria would afford him what Croydon wouldn't: fame and fortune.

After he'd showered and shaved, he felt a little more like himself again, and the unease and nausea resided. He slipped into his Tommy Hilfiger jeans and straightened his Ray-bans in the bedroom mirror. With just a dab of wet-look gel to spike his closely cropped hair, the final act in his morning grooming routine, before peeling on a Diesel T-shirt that made a second skin, he exited. Jack, as always, in search of the looker in the room but unable to get Anna completely off his mind.

III

TERRY

Terry hated travelling. But then again, he'd hated everything since Anna left him. He fiddled with engines for hours on end so that others could travel and not him. Travel far away from their problems. He had understood engines like he understood little else in life. Understood them since the age of fifteen.

The older he got the less he understood of his brief time with Anna too. Terry hadn't figured out why a woman like Anna had ever shown him the slightest interest.

But she had.

She had made him love her.

He almost hated her for it. And perhaps he could concede that in some deep, raked and stony part of his closed heart he did hate the woman who had shown him a possible life, a wonderful life, and then ejected him so cruelly out of it and back to his simplified world of clanging metal, oil, sparks and wires. Engines and only engines were a big part of his uninspired journey through a used-up feeling of middle-aged life.

He'd finally reached his destination in the here and now, and an end to perpetual motion.

Terry had only been in this part of the world once before to service cable cars. He'd forgotten its bare natural beauty and its pure snow-capped landscapes.

"No, I'll take those," Terry snatched his luggage back from an over-keen porter as if the guy were a thief. What sort of a man had his cases carried up by a skinny runt of a kid barely out of school? It was insulting. Terry grunted and the millennial, too young to shave, nodded like an obedient pupil at the refusal, the kid's eyes bright and his smile one of eagerness. Terry resented the awkwardness of moments like this.

There were postcards on sale in reception and he bought one on impulse. Jens, the manager of the Hoppermeyer hotel-come-motel, informed him the name of his hotel was taken from his surname. He announced this with pride, smiling with a mouth full of metal teeth matching the octagonal gold of his professor-like spectacles.

Jens' English may have been as clearly pronounced as the Queen's but his personality was verging on the robotic as if his Berlitz lesson had never quite finished but ran on into reality.

Anna had stepped around difficult vowels the way Chopin played difficult notes.

Anna's spirit was everywhere in Austria.

He did have a tender side and Anna had revealed it to him. But not without resentment and a touch of self-loathing.

He'd only know how he felt for sure when he laid eyes on her again. If it didn't work out then he'd come back here and do some sightseeing before he left.

"Here for the skiing?"

Terry shook his head, leaving it hanging as to what he was here for. It was none of his business and Jens finally got the message. Terry was unconcerned about offending an Austrian Norman Bates. The Bates Motel took its name from a surname too. That's what freaky hotel-motel owners did. Named their motel-hotels after themselves.

Just don't put me into cabin number one, Terry laughed to himself.

Unfortunately, soon the reality of that would not seem quite so funny to him. Not funny at all.

Only psychopaths found murder funny.

IV

TONY

The voice in his head had stopped, and that was something. He couldn't bear risking madness again. Not after the last time.

But without Anna, his life seemed soulless, desperate and directionless.

Tony was lost again, he had to concentrate. He was on alpine back roads that rose and fell and twisted in and out, ending in sharp hairpin bends that could make tiredness fatal.

As he thrashed through the gears of his Honda CR-V and revved the engine, he made an effort to calm himself. He and this car were completely at odds with each other again. Some of the S-bends ahead had crumbled away with time and harsh weather, desperately in need of resurfacing.

A persistently nagging inner voice warned him that he hadn't seen a single vehicle in miles.

He'd been warned by the Avis man that his Honda C-V had no snow chains or "Schneeketten" as they called them. The road sign he'd just passed displayed a white tyre on a blue background indicating that this was a route to avoid. He backed up and took the lower road he'd somehow missed the first time. Rubbing his eyes, Tony was relieved to see a little lay-by up ahead in which to pull into. He desperately needed to get back on the autobahn which lurked somewhere far below, but these treacherous mountain roads were not leading him down to it.

"Not there," Tony said to himself, rubbing his tired eyes. "You're not there."

He couldn't see her yet but he could hear Anna humming the chorus of a nursery rhyme, finding her way back into his distorted reality.

Anna emerged dressed in her usual black dress and veil, completely ignorant of the weather conditions. Anna always wore the same black funeral dress, her veil thin enough to disclose a pretty freckled face.

He'd seen her like the walking dead for weeks now. All his other visions lost to the power of this one horrific image.

Tony put his hands to his head like a primate and screwed his eyes up. "Not there. You don't exist," he screamed.

He looked.

Anna was gone. Mountains and silence in every direction.

Tony reprogrammed the sat nav for what must have been the ninth or tenth time. No satellite signal and no toneless female voice to reassuringly guide him back to civilisation greeted him.

Tony scowled at the inadequate Tourist Information map, this road joined the autobahn somewhere, but he'd been on it half an hour already.

Anna reappeared, walking on the other side of the mountain. She was walking down the sheer drop of the mountainside vertically, defying gravity like an astronaut on a space-walk before disappearing out of sight.

After a minute of silence, Anna emerged climbing up onto the road ten feet away from Tony's hire car, calling out for his help. Her desperate eyes locked on his under the funeral veil.

"No!"

Anna was completely silent this time. Eerily silent.

"God no!"

Tony scrunched up his eyes, hearing a car door open.

When Tony opened his eyes, a trembling ghostlike Anna sat in the passenger seat next to him as if they were lovers again, reaching out to touch him.

Her mascara ran in tears of black dirt and brick coloured clay clung to her dishevelled dress and neck as if she'd climbed out of her own grave.

"Don't get into the car," Anna said. "When you see me at the house, don't get into that car, Tony. If you do, he'll kill everyone, you understand? You're my best hope, if you survive then you'll use your gift to unmask him. I know you will. I believe in your gift. I believe in you, Tony."

"Jesus," Tony said with a shudder as she faded away. "Jesus fucking Christ!"

She reappeared momentarily, stretching out a hand. "Don't get into that car," Anna screamed. Tony shut his eyes. After a few minutes of hearing only his heavy breathing, Tony believed Anna had vanished for good this time.

"What's happening to me?" Tony asked no one, in tears. He could not stop his hand from shaking for several minutes.

Tony had a head for figures that was a curse. A "head for figures" was how his proud mother had described his precocious mathematical ability. She had also described it as a "gift from God" but Tony disagreed, a gift could be returned.

Tony preferred to call it "his ability." An ability that had taken him far just as his mother said it would. Tony's "head for figures" had taken him out of a council house to a full scholarship at Cambridge and a plush job in a blue-chip company at twenty-one. The starting salary of eighty grand a year in an investment bank, a millionaire at twenty-four turned into a six-point-two million tax-free fortune at thirty.

In reality, Tony only had an average mathematical ability. He'd known this since he was a child. What he had was the ability to see into the past and future at times. He could predict things of significance, actually seeing them unravel. Only he had no control over it and he eventually learned, with considerable bitterness, that material wealth was the only way he could profit from it since he couldn't change these visions.

So, Tony hid his ability behind a "head for figures" and a lucrative career as a financier transporting him away from being the walking freak show that had been his childhood trying to make sense of his gift.

The figure that counted was the £250 bottle of Bollinger champagne that led him to date the most beautiful girl he'd ever laid his eyes on – Anna.

The final figure would be this year's date on his gravestone, for Tony had the Devil on his back for how he'd used his gift. His tricks unfolding before his sleep-deprived eyes on a nightly basis. Death was close now.

Anna had been the first to call "his ability" by its proper scientific name, ESP – Extra Sensory Perception. She was also the first to point out that people throughout history had lived full lives with such an ability, a little bit of "peeking behind the curtains" as she put it. She never tried to tell him how to best use it. That's what made her so special.

"You're still my special guy," Anna said, reaching out to stroke his forehead.

Tony's eyes were wide open as he crossed himself. "Hail Mary mother of God."

A hoot rang out around the mountainside and Anna disappeared.

Another hoot and an amiable, presentable looking young couple pulled over and stepped out to take photos of the view.

Tony saw that they were young, very young. Students perhaps and very much in love and this only had the effect of reviving his longing for Anna. They'd been kids too when they had fallen in love.

"God bless you," Tony said to the French couple when they offered to let him follow their Range Rover down. "I thought I'd be left up here."

Back on the autobahn, and its familiar steady unbroken flow of traffic and tarmac, Tony felt a relieved man. The A13 autobahn sign announced Igls was ten kilometres and Innsbruck fourteen.

His hotel-come-lodge was typically set, perched scenically in the hills.

The view from all sides was unforgettable in every way. Everything untouched by commercial development up here, everything lightly sprinkled and dusted with snow. Postcard perfect, fit to grace the front cover of any guidebook to Austria. It lifted his spirits, but not for long.

The medication was losing its power over him and his reality evaporating with it.

The visionary Anna in the black dress wasn't after him yet, but she would be back shortly. He'd get an hour of peace, maybe two if he was lucky.

Tony didn't know how he was going to explain this vision to Anna when he met up with her, but he would think of something. Maybe she wanted more than friendship. Tony had enough money to not have a time limit on his stay here and all he needed to trade was an internet connection. He had nothing to go back to, and at this moment looking out over the hills of perhaps the most beautiful setting of his thirty-seven mostly unexciting years, Tony had never felt more alive.

I've nothing left to lose now, he thought.

He was soon to realise just how wrong he was.

V

DENNIS

It was in all the papers. He'd brought a copy of both *The Telegraph* and *The Times on Sunday* in the departure lounge. He always remained loyal to these two because he had friends who wrote for both and he admired the editorial discipline to relate researched fact over all too easy sensationalism. Truth being stranger than fiction, no writer would have imagined such a daring feat as he was currently reading.

If he'd written a plot like this the critics would have never shut up about it. The body on the stage throughout the entire first act. The fact that the crime fitted perfectly with the plot of the play again would have been too convenient for the critics.

All yours, Chief Inspector. Dennis chuckled to himself. *Your final case Dawson old boy.*

The police were concentrating on the tense atmosphere amongst the cast and crew because no-one outside this professional circle could have had the opportunity to poison the actor's glass. It was possible but highly unlikely that a member of the public had snuck through the surely numerous security measures in place.

The news had the case on every channel at the airport.

The scandal that half of the cream of the London theatre was being detained and under suspicion for the crime was sweeping the nation. He'd overheard a conversation in the terminal that the bookies were even taking bets on who the guilty party was.

"Would you mind?" A smiling star-struck woman thrust a copy of one of his Chief Inspector Dawson novels at him.

"My pleasure," Dennis said, recognizing the smiling teenage girl with braces as the woman's daughter. "And where are you off to?"

"New York," the girl said excitedly, her braces glinting as she spoke.

"New York, wow," Dennis picked up his book enthusiastically, all six hundred and fifty pages of it. "That's a long flight though. You'll nearly be through this."

He removed his silver Parker pen from his top pocket, signing an autograph in the departure lounge to the young girl and her mother who had bought his latest novel, *The Piper's Rat*, in Gatwick's WH Smith.

"Who's Anna?"

"Sorry?"

He'd signed it to Anna instead of Suzanna before rectifying the mistake with the beginnings of a boyish flush.

"I apologise for being flustered," Dennis said as he wrote. "Pretty ladies always have that effect on me, I'm afraid."

"Christine's your number one fan." The mother beamed.

Dennis winced at the cliché.

And what about his motivation for coming all this way, he thought as he attempted *The Times* crossword puzzle with a clear head and a gin and tonic on the plane. No critic would have bought it in his fiction. And yet here he was. But nobody who had met Anna, his Anna, could have questioned his sanity in doing so.

Men, women, boys and girls always wanted what they couldn't have. The thrill of the chase it gave. It was so basic and yet so compelling. Compelling enough to last a lifetime.

He didn't feel like watching an in-flight movie, and instead, he chuckled away at episodes of *The Simpsons* he'd already seen and *Lee Evans Live* stamping around on stage.

The man next to him turned pages of *The Da Vinci Code* with quiet businessman-like dignity he admired and envied as a fellow author. A woman in the aisle seat in front rapidly clicked through her romance novel on her Kindle.

Dennis felt that the best books described what you already knew about the human condition.

Dennis looked out of the plane window to watch a patchwork quilt of countryside unravel itself below him, stretches of barren countryside stitched to the rich bottle greens of a forest. The sun glinted off the metal wing, catching Dennis' formal-looking expression reflected in a glorious intensification of light. Somebody at a party had told him once he'd been given the face of everyman. The rest of the group speculating that that was perhaps why he'd become a writer, too wrapped up in observation to participate and contest the role of the Alpha male. It was why he'd spent long spells of his life single. And that was certainly the case, until Anna.

Anna had given him courage, passion and self-confidence after only a few days of their meeting. She'd given him the best months of his life, and she'd done it effortlessly. He'd never met anyone on stage, screen or real life who could come close to her elegant charisma. She was the only woman he'd ever known who knew what you were thinking before you knew it yourself.

To more simple-minded people this would have threatened them, her superior probing intellect, but to him, he felt unburdened by it. He'd been the geeky straight-A kid at school, the misfit at uni and the prodigious writer in adulthood. Her honed emotional intelligence that could have only come from the most insightful of upbringings ended his isolation.

She could have done anything, he believed, and more than that she could make whoever was in the room with her seem like they could do anything.

This rare quality was what made you wonder if love could, in fact, last an eternity and if you could ever die while it lasted.

She'd got his early work too. She'd seen through the veil of endless philosophy that had scarred and mutilated his prose. Got it and loved it. Keeping faith with all its laden intellectualism and heavy scepticism of a world which he feared he was rapidly losing touch with.

When she'd left him so suddenly, he'd felt completely devastated. He wrote nothing of note for three years. He did nothing of note for three years, apart from packing on twenty pounds in weight. Pounds he'd still not entirely shifted and was glad of the multiple layers the Alps necessitated. But it was still him. Still the Dennis Harker she'd fallen in love with.

There was just this jealous ex to uncover. She'd told him something once. Something that made Dennis suspect this man was a sociopath from a young age. A sociopath she'd cared for despite what he'd done to her life.

"What he was still doing to it," he said to himself quietly. "Poor Anna."

But there was no record of such a person when he'd put a private detective on the case. The same private detective who'd failed to find Anna shortly afterwards when she'd disappeared.

Throughout their fling, he had got the impression that this ex was one of those creatures that only observed life from a distance. Someone who would fit into society only for some self-serving end and would never risk coming close enough to be spotted. The pattern of their diligent stalker went beyond the jealous type, so far at the wrong end of the scale of abnormal behaviour in every facet of his personality to be brilliant. His whole life an act.

"Murderers have no small talk," Dennis muttered to himself, scribbling this thought down on a paper napkin. The detail seemed important. "No small talk."

Dennis spied a stunning brunette and for a moment, the briefest of glimpsed moments, she was Anna.

His mind settled on what Anna had said, what he'd forced out of her one late rainy day near the end of their love affair. A love affair that had been uniquely theirs and up until that point an unblemished paradise of fresh still being discovered affection. An exciting love. True love.

She left him with no doubt that this man, the man that had stalked them to their rudely interrupted Rome vacation was a dangerous psychopath.

"A real 'bad egg' in Dawson speak."

Anna had laughed.

"Would Dawson be able to catch him though?"

"Listen, Dawson knows his shoe size, that he's left-handed and likes his steak medium-rare. The guy doesn't stand a chance."

Anna laughed again. "That's how he'll catch him?"

"That's how he'll catch him, the clever old bastard."

The reality had been different.

VI

JEFF

The coach driver attacked another S-bend, dropping gear and hooting before ploughing ahead like a driver who'd spent his life gauging the relationship between slanting road and heavy vehicle on these monstrous corners. These tight, blind bends made every corner a potential death trap just avoided.

Jeff counted four Skodas in a row to ease his nerves.

Tratzberg peered around the bend, unravelling in layers of mountain wood and sloping town.

He was staying in a newly opened, moderately sized inn somewhere far below the Renaissance landmark of the Schloss Tratzberg. The Schloss, an imposing castle, he could make out in the distance. The coach was currently winding its way on another ascent of a tight S-bend around the mountainside, the destination of Tratzberg although visible getting no closer.

The guide book he flicked through was way out of date, comically so.

His Chelsea hoodie attracted the attention of the only other English-speaking person on the bus, a pretty but very pregnant woman named Alice, who perched herself opposite him and seemed determined to tell him her life story. He'd felt guilty about running out on his fiancé Debbie as it was, and he could have done without this girl telling him about how her last boyfriend had abandoned her and didn't need another reason to feel even more like the callous shit he already knew himself to be. She was returning to her Austrian mother, the mother whom she hoped would take her in and forgive her for leaving home. That was the impression he got.

She still didn't know if her unborn child was a boy or a girl. If it was a girl, she was going to call it Amanda or Chloe and if it was a boy, Stephen or Jonathon.

Jeff smiled politely throughout a monologue threatening tears with each quivering word, wondering what he'd done to deserve this.

Ditching your bride to be virtually at the altar probably tops the list, Jeff. This girl is a message sent from above.

"That's a real shame," Jeff said for what felt like the hundredth inadequate time.

Jeff helped Alice with her bags when she got off at her stop, a village below Tratzberg about the size of a supermarket car park.

Jeff continued nodding politely, not listening as she slowly disappeared from his life like every other woman he'd met since Anna.

"Anna," Jeff said, trying it on for size. He had the printed email invitation in his trouser pocket. Who said he wasn't a romantic? He'd read it enough times to have already crumpled it. "I want you too, my love," he whispered to himself.

Jeff waved to Alice from the coach window.

He'd genuinely felt sorry for the girl, recognising that she was talking to ease the building nervous tension inside of her. The mother took her luggage, her greeting not much warmer than the weather.

Jeff put the email invitation back in his jeans pocket, resisting re-reading it as the coach pulled away.

What're you doing here, mate? Jeff asked himself. *You should be at your wedding.*

Brian, his deserted best man, would be doing his nut. And then there was his mother to consider. Debbie's mother didn't even bear thinking about, and his father? Jesus Christ, he might as well do a Ronnie Biggs and not go back at all at this rate. Jeff certainly felt as if he was a fleeing criminal with what he'd done and his reputation in his local probably just as notorious as Ronnie Biggs by now.

He laughed to himself. *Jeff Biggsy Yates.*

Jeff rubbed his hands together, blowing warmth on them.

He was still in love with Anna, and that was all that mattered in the end. Love. When love came your way in this world you just had to snatch it.

Better to pull out now than lead Debbie on and get her in the same delicate situation as that poor girl. Jeff felt relieved Debbie was out of his life and Anna was back in the picture.

Only no one would see it his way, Jeff was sure. Not until they met Anna themselves would they understand. Anna turned minds as well as heads.

VII

PATRICK

Patrick gradually moved in newly formed queues out onto the busy Herzog-Friedrich-Strasse passing multicoloured Baroque buildings that made this old district of Innsbruck resemble a toy town. The sun was high in the sky but too weak to melt the snow underfoot.

"Excuse me?" Patrick said, stopping two young women passing by. They looked like locals to him although you could never tell for sure. "Where's the Helblinghaus, bitte? Nehmen sie Strasse?"

They laughed at the mixed-in English and botched German.

"Just down there," one of them replied. "Can't miss it."

"Danke Schoen."

They replied, "no problem," and carried on walking, looking back and laughing. Patrick waved and they burst into giggles again.

The bright sunshine made him forget the more sinister side of his obsessive motive in coming here. His sessions over the years with his patients had disclosed that rejection from a lover was the ugliest emotion by some distance with what it contained to turn a perfectly normal human being into. Crimes of passion were not uncommon throughout the ages, and passion to someone else was almost a crime at times. Patrick hoped more than anything this wasn't such an occasion with himself. Another rejection to live with.

A chill wind caught him with the accompanying thought, and he was glad that he'd packed more than one of the roll-neck paisley sweaters he was wearing like a billboard to his profession.

He'd needed this little excursion, and yet his reasons for taking it were never far from his conscience. He'd never been out of love with Anna, he accepted now. And acceptance was the stable base of all psychology. But he was lying to himself: he had to know and would risk everything for it, even his own life.

Maybe this emotion would bring him closer to the personality that had summoned him here.

That was a funny way to put it, he thought then as he sat and ordered a Stella beer at a quaint little cafe on Hofgasse that afforded him a view of both the Stadtturm tower, like something out of Tolkien's *Lord of the Rings* in this weird quest across this mountainous region and the Helblinghaus. The Helblinghaus's swirls of detailed Rocco stuccowork spoke of the grotesque eighteenth-century opulence that intimidated all the gaudily painted buildings around, making them appear like mere beach huts at the seaside in their lack of comparative charm. The divide between the rich and the poor evident where ever you looked.

The local he'd hired his skis from informed him that the destination for this party was a spectacular one. The Wentworth Lodge, a Victorian mansion built by a Samuel Wentworth, an eccentric shipping millionaire in the days of the unchallenged British Empire and before the world had gone through two world wars and countless recessions. Wentworth, after three unsuccessful and reputedly unsavoury marriages with young local beauties, had died up there looking down at the world, isolated and alone, his leg chopped off with gangrene set in.

"And it's not far you say?"

"Five kilometres. Most of it up," the local said, pointing his finger to the sky and pronouncing the word up as 'opp'. "That is the least of your problems, my friend."

Patrick eventually understood what the local had meant when he saw the lodge house for himself in the distance with his binoculars. The south side of the house was carved into the mountainside.

The new owner was a mystery to everyone except that he must have acquired a fortune in something to have bought this opulent retreat and still have his identity remain undisclosed.

The cable car running guests up to the house must have cost a fortune in itself to run, Patrick was informed. The whole set-up seemed ridiculous to him now, a party in the middle of nowhere. At Christmas, no less.

Well, there wasn't a more seasonal setting than this, he supposed.

Patrick cautiously skied down the three-kilometre trail leading back to the town, heading for the bar across the street from his hotel. His intention had been only to take a snoop at the place and establish that it did exist. From the way the locals described the Wentworth Mansion, Patrick feared it might have only been part of folklore and another wild goose chase.

Patrick sipped his beer, ordered another. He did so on the persuasive advice of the infectiously cheerful waiter, exhibiting all the unguarded extroversion of youth and wondering inquisitiveness. He settled on the recommended Pilsner beer, a stronger and less bitter brew than the Stella he'd become accustomed to.

Patrick flipped through his guidebook as he drank. He wanted to see Hofburg Palace and Dom St. Jakob before setting off on his ascent to this luxurious retreat and a descent into the mind of this stalking madman he'd finally get to confront.

There was a part of him treating this day as if it were his last, and he of all people knew that was not a healthy state to be in. Not healthy at all.

Chasing a past love was not healthy, and yet the mere thought that he would set his eyes on his Anna again after all these years, to touch her, to smell her hair… no, he would not permit himself the fall into this self-indulgence; he needed focus now. With that thought, Patrick finished his beer, rewarded the waiter with his biggest tip of the season, and strolled back to a hotel that was little more than a hostel with a dining hall.

Patrick would finish this once and for all and live out the remainder of his life free of its burden and the sleepless nights it had brought.

Patrick looked around, fearful that someone might know his every move, and it was quite plausible that he was being watched right now. He looked around at fifty possible suspects never feeling so helplessly vulnerable or more of a foreigner.

VIII

GRACE

Every part of her ached and she longed for the simple act of brushing her teeth. Travelling always gave her that lingering nauseous taste that sat in her mouth no matter how many diet sodas she sipped. She would chew sugar-free gum as her dentist recommended, but it was no real substitute and upset her empty stomach anyhow. She knew from her medical expertise that chewing without food and sipping diet soda combined to produce acid that sat irritably in the gut.

More than brushing her teeth, Grace longed for a long hot soapy bath and a glass of red wine. Oh, that would be a heavenly combination to pamper herself.

When the shuddering plane touched down on the runway of the Innsbruck-Kranebitten Airport, Grace was relieved and surprised that her ears hadn't popped like they usually did and wondered if this were due to exceptional flying, reduced air cabin pressure, or an inexplicable aberration of medical science.

Her chalet was less than thirty minutes from the airport and she soon had her wish fulfilled of that long hot, soapy bath she'd been anticipating the whole flight. Her suite was decorated without flair but with taste, and the balcony that she stepped out onto greeted her with an instant wall of refreshing coolness as she took in a breath of unpolluted alpine air, a welcome reinvigoration after the energy-sapping heat of the bath.

She sipped a glass of a wine she'd found in the minibar. A wine that was a little too fruity for her taste to be truly delicious, the sort of wine you'd find for a couple of euros in a supermarket even, but still a welcome aperitif nevertheless.

Grace hadn't visited Innsbruck since she was a schoolgirl, and she felt excited, longing to ski again. But the thought of Anna and this stalking maniac had tinged the exoticness of her keen-for-adventure spirit.

After a lunch of a filling baguette spiced with a cheese tang she'd liked, Grace sat on the terrace of an Innsbruck cafe where she was promptly served by a pleasant waitress in a decorative bow-tie. Grace knew that Eiskaffee was iced coffee with ice cream and whipped cream, but recognised little else aside from Cappuccino and Milchkaffee. She'd ordered a Mazagran just to be adventurous before the waitress warned her that this was not regular coffee at all, this coffee came served with an ice cube and was laced with rum, to be drunk in a single gulp. Not what she wanted at all.

The waitress suggested that it was probably Konsul Grace should go for, which she explained with great care was simply strong black coffee with a dash of crème to act as a coolant to her taste buds.

"Looks like it'll have to be a Konsul then," Grace said, beaming a smile she hoped wasn't construed as too flirtatious. Grace ordered an apfelstrudel, patting her waistline with a guilty effect which amused the waitress.

"Can't drink coffee without a pastry to sweeten it," Grace said.

"Of course not," the waitress replied. "Who could?"

"I'm a doctor," Grace said. "And an actress in my spare time."

And now Grace knew she was flirting.

Grace stroked her fringe, nodding to the building behind her. "I'm staying across the street."

"I'm a waitress... obviously," the waitress smiled, subconsciously fumbling her wedding ring. "And a married woman."

"Oh, I didn't mean," Grace said with embarrassment, but she had already moved onto the next table to take another order, looking back with a playful smile.

On a pleasantly full stomach and a mild sugar rush, Grace walked in and out of gift shops taking in both the people and the merchandise. Leaving a small shopping arcade, she noticed the man in the mirror sunglasses again she suspected was following her.

He disappeared as soon as Grace attempted to take his picture on her mobile phone.

She returned to her chalet, double-checking all the suite's windows and doors were locked.

Grace fell into a deep but troubled slumber with the aid of self-prescribed sleeping tablets, knowing tomorrow she'd go up into the mountains to a remote house where a party awaited her.

And Anna.

IX

SIMON

Wherever he went today people were giving him anxious, uncertain smiles. Surely his imagination playing tricks with his reality.
This is what it felt like to be a fugitive. Everybody who met his eye a potential plainclothes police officer moving in for an arrest. Every tourist snapping away on their digital cameras an opportunist pap looking for a scoop.

Simon was relieved to find that the young man he thought may have recognised him on the train was only after him to take a photograph, but was not assertive enough to ask straight out.

"Press this one, please," he said, extending the hand with his Samsung Galaxy phone in.

A relieved looking Simon took the picture and left.

He was glad to be off the Eurostar train and in the company of a taxi driver who'd in all likelihood never heard of the West End or the name Simon Stevens. It reassured him again in his present incognito existence.

He'd bought a copy of *The Daily Express* at St. Pancras and saw a picture of himself and the other infamous celeb suspects. It had an element of the surreal about it as if it were a reality TV show. On page four his disappearance was opposite a column speculating on the likelihood of Britney Spears' latest comeback being a success. Any publicity was good publicity as his director and agent had been citing all week. But when you're the chief suspect in a murder inquiry that wasn't necessarily the truth.

As Simon shaved, he squared his shoulders and took himself in. At thirty-nine, his features were still sharp but his eyes were too close together and his nose too long to support any realistic ambitions of ever becoming a matinee idol. The acting profession was still modelling in this regard. His jaw-line not strong enough to ever be associated with the lead in action movies. The best you could say about his looks was that they were conventional. And so, his agent had agreed with him when he'd said his best hope would be to become the "everyman" of his generation. The type of actor the audience could instantly recognise and identify with no matter the role. A modern-day Jimmy Stewart.

That was his agent's advice. His friend Christian disagreed. Christian's advice had been that he needed a new agent and fast. An everyman could also be a no one. A blur to a casting director searching out a strong definable personality.

Simon thought about this as he began to shape his disguise, his features pigeon-holed into the "everyman" he'd finally turn to his advantage.

The features staring back at him moulded into this everyman facelessness. He shaved off his thick brown hair without regret until a smooth, pink dome appeared. The best everyman haircut that was available to him. He was surprised at how pale the skin underneath his scalp appeared; he'd considered himself to be tanned.

"Welcome to your new life, Simon." He smiled to himself. "Who loves ya, baby!"

No more anxious moments.

Not today. Christian, the play's director, would do his nut if he saw what he was doing now. He was already playing a guy fifteen years younger than himself in the 1950s. It made him chuckle. The Lex Luther look. It'd grow back in the two-week break. Not enough to appease his director, but Christian would just have to live with it.

But would he go back?

A new man. Simon said to himself, running his hands over the smooth dome and excited by the new look.

The sights of Innsbruck hardly moved him, almost an anti-climax. He'd already seen the tourist stops on previous visits, and so Simon gathered his luggage and headed out to where he understood the Wentworth mansion to be. In the middle of nowhere.

It would be better to be cheeky and stay with Anna tonight than to book a hotel room under a false name.

To his surprise, the taxi would only take him as far as a Schtzhutte, which turned out to be a tiny, snow-bound hut. The Schtzhutte the only building to be seen for miles around in this deep woodland area nestled between two mountain peaks.

He was informed by the Schtzhutte attendee in the most rudimentary broken English that this point onwards was private property. There was a cable car, also private property, a half a mile up to his desired location which he could just about see looming above a few hundred feet of bare rock face heavily blanketed by snow.

The cable car was useless unless you had the verification code to get past the surrounding wire cage, he was told. Or rather worked out from what the man was saying. When Simon told him this was fine, he was expected and had been given the code, the local still tried to persuade him not to go any further.

The cable car was not used regularly, Simon was warned again in functional English more sign language than words.

"When was the last time you saw somebody use it?" Simon asked.

"People they use it, yah. Somebody like you, yah?"

"Like me? British, you mean?"

The attendant nodded, "yah."

You had to climb two hills and a half a mile of backwoods forestry to get to the cable car, an enclosed area in which the attendant had warned Simon to be on his guard for wolves.

The unmanned car itself, a space-age silver-grey, had a sign warning that no more than eight persons at a time could be in the car, and could hold a maximum of one metric tonne in weight, including luggage. Simon knew his weight to be a year-round eighty-five kilograms and his luggage a meagre twenty.

Simon was about to brave the ascent alone when a woman appeared. A slim, refined woman. A woman he'd momentarily mistaken for Anna. But only momentarily. This woman seemed older, more reserved. But still desirable.

Most women couldn't measure up to Anna in height, weight, looks, perceptiveness or any other desirable attribute that a man instinctually assesses as a kind of selective beauty contest in his mind on acquaintance.

This woman, a doctor, was also one of Anna's guests.

Grace had the same activation code for the car as him, he discovered. Simon punched it in and their ascent began.

With each passing moment, as the cable car drew closer to the house, and the distance between ground and car increased to a fatal height that tested his nerve, Simon grew more expectant of what was to come.

The doctor, Grace, not wanting to look down, closed her eyes. Simon found her hand grasping his. Her other hand seemed welded to the handrail.

It was an intimate moment in which they seemed to know each other in another lifetime.

"Thanks," she said, unable to raise the smile she wanted to give him.

"Just keep looking up, you'll be fine."

It proved to be a good tip. The Alps were all around them, framed in glass. They didn't look real with their picture-perfect sprinkling of whiteness, as if it were a green screen projection, a flawless dream world that would dissipate if you got too close.

When they reached the house, Simon politely hauled Grace's luggage over the snow buried steps and dropped them in the grand but empty foyer. Simon momentarily left her alone, doubling back for his luggage. Grace decided she couldn't wait and disappeared in search of their host.

It would prove to be a long search. A very long search.

X

ANNA

Another day.

Or night.

No food, no water, no light, no sound.

No one.

Anna felt like weeping but didn't have the moisture left in her tear ducts to do so. Her face felt dry and dusty to the touch and Anna wondered if she was still beautiful.

Maybe it's because I'm beautiful that got me into this situation. This masked psycho probably spent hours looking over pictures of me on billboards, in magazines and my TV ads.

Being beautiful had got her nowhere in life, nowhere except here.

Anna tried not to think of the Ryan Reynolds movie she'd rented a couple of months back and how his captor had at least left him with a mobile phone to contact the outside world. But this fear was leaving her now.

A large part of her retreating psyche felt nothing except the rough, gritty stone of her entombment on her bleeding hands. In her emotional fatigue, the darkness was primitively comforting. Like a wounded animal she would rest in it.

I'm not an animal.

"Let me out!" Anna coughed more than screamed with a sudden unexpected jolt of fury that welled up from deep within her.

She pounded her prison walls with her knuckles for several seconds, not feeling the pain. All of her fingernails had snagged off in her last scratching outburst.

"You hear me, you creep? Fucking let me out!"

There was no answer. The only sound came from her laboured breaths.

Anna knew she'd never leave here alive.

To Die For

"I've no doubt in my own mind that we have been invited here by a madman – probably a dangerous homicidal lunatic."

Agatha Christie, *And Then There Were None*

PART 2

The First Night Together

CHAPTER TWO

I

"All right then. Likes or dislikes first?" Patrick said.

"Why don't we do both together?" Grace replied.

"All right, I'll go first then," Patrick said. "Likes. Restoring cars and winning money at poker."

"Dislikes?" Grace asked for them all.

"Losing money at poker." Patrick looked searchingly across the dinner table. "I'll pass to oh... Jeff, I think," Patrick said, taking another sip of his Perrier.

"Okay, likes..." Jeff raised his glass, getting up out of his seat to address the rest of the table. "Champagne, parties, having a good time." Jeff sat back down, slumping into his chair. "Dislikes. Marriage, commitment, responsibility. You get the picture."

"Any kids, Jeff?" Patrick inquired.

"None that I know of. Like everyone else here I'm childless, don't you find that a bit odd?" Jeff looked around contemplating this. "Before I depress everybody in the room with my life, I'll pass to you, Doctor."

"Likes are... let me see... money, don't we all? Running." Grace took a long pause. "Theatre, watching rugby, acting class and champagne, as you may have guessed." Grace shared a conspirator's smile with everyone at the table, replacing a stray lock of hair. "Dislikes? Being put on the spot." She looked around accusingly at Jeff. "And men who can't take no for an answer."

"That's all men," Dennis quipped, coming into the room with four brandies and a G&T on a tray.

Grace elbowed Jack, seated to her right. "You're up, Romeo."

"Jack likes..." Jack said straight out, taking a chocolate mint from the middle of the table and unwrapping it, "any sport or exercise you can think of." He raised a suggestive smile for Grace. "In or outdoors."

"Jack dislikes... women who play head games and people who think they're better than you. No, wait, people who think they're better than you because they went to a private school. Ronnie?"

"Likes would be teaching." Ronnie put up a hand. "I know I know, it's boring but... Dislikes would be substitute teachers and skiing. Tony."

"If you haven't guessed by now, reading is my main like. Reading Dennis Harker books, I suppose."

Tony was interrupted by jeers "Suck up", "Shut up" and "Ass-kisser" from the rest of the table.

"Don't criticise the man for good taste," Dennis laughed. "Now let him finish."

"Dislikes. Romance novels, internet dating and hotels without hot water. Dennis."

"You like my books but dislike me then?"

"No-no, I meant you're up next."

"I know what you meant. I was just kidding. You've got to learn to lighten up around me." Dennis rattled the cutlery with chimes for dramatic effect. "Likes. Cooking. Not one of you thought to mention my cooking as one of your likes?" Dennis looked around the table. "Guess not. I won't hold it against you."

"Just get on with it. Dislikes?"

"That's easy, critics."

They all laughed at his joke this time.

Dennis looked around the table. "That leaves er... Simon, I guess."

"Don't be shy," Grace smiled. "We've all bared our souls. Whatever revelation you have, now's the time."

"Likes. I don't know. Keeping fit, watching movies. Bergman, Polanski, Kubrick." Simon smiled at Grace. "Acting class."

"Any dislikes?" Patrick asked.

"None, don't have any."

"Bullshit," Jeff said.

"Who's left?" Patrick inquired.

"No one," Jeff said. "We've all had our turn."

"Well," Patrick said, "With Anna not here, why don't we do hers for her?"

To Die For

"Okay," Jack said. "This'll be fun. Likes, parties, night clubs, exotic photo-shoots."

"Spending money, don't forget that," Grace said.

"Other people's money," Tony added with a smile, gesturing at the fine house they were in.

"Yachts, Casinos, famous friends," Grace reminded them, swigging more champagne from the bottle and passing it back to Jeff.

"Men with tattoos," Jack said.

"Men without tattoos," Patrick said. "Intellectuals, art."

"You can add my cooking," Dennis finished. "But probably not my books, if I'm honest."

"Nobody likes your books, mate," Jeff added. "When are you going to wake up to that? No one's even read them."

"I've changed my mind," Dennis declared. "Dislikes, critics and Jeff."

"Don't listen to him, everyone. Trust me, he doesn't know what he's talking about," Tony beamed at the others and then Dennis, "I've read them all. And like I say, I'm his number one fan!"

II

It was Patrick who approached the delicate subject that had been behind all these awkward anecdotes when they all burst forth with their stories of this blackmailing ex. A couple of minutes later the room became ominously silent.

They were all exes themselves, of course; there seemed some kind of showdown in that fact all of a sudden. Jeff made the most out of the now absent Grace being an ex of Anna's but was cut off by Patrick with the look of a disapproving father. *Although there were only ten years between them*, Dennis thought with amusement. *Patrick looked and acted like he could be either Jeff's or Jack's father.*

Ronnie and Patrick were the only two not drinking, and the only two who seemed concerned by their being lured out here to this mysterious location with an absent host. Dennis had shared this sentiment an hour ago but the G&Ts he had knocked back since had taken the edge off his inquisitive mind.

There was safety in numbers, and in the alcohol, they knocked back, but not in the complacency held by both.

But Patrick, like the rest of them, was helpless until Anna arrived.

Dennis met his thoughtful gaze with an equally uneasy look of his own across the dinner table. He was not the only one unsettled by all of this. And in that very fear was the thought that it wouldn't be the Anna they once knew and loved who was going to show up, it would be somebody else altogether. They were not to know yet just how right they were.

Chapter Three

I

As dessert was about to be eaten, the defrosted ready-made supermarket Gugelhupf they'd waited nearly half an hour for, they continued to chat with an ease none of them felt.

Gugelhupf turned out to be a light sponge cake that was only gross sounding, not tasting. Dennis informed Patrick that Gugelhupf was said to be Sigmund Freud's favourite dessert. He served it for eight.

"Freud did some of his finest thinking with Gugelhupf in his belly," Dennis said, smiling as he divided up the rich pudding onto plates.

"Is that right?" Patrick replied, tucking in.

"Wasn't it Freud who said he wanted to fuck his own mother?" Jack said.

"Not in so many words." They all laughed except Grace.

Grace was the first to notice the cable car moving across the east side bay window where they were eating, raising the expectation that it might be their hostess. "Someone else is coming. Look."

A wall of glass from floor to ceiling offered a breathtaking view of the Alps and the slow-moving cable car making its ascent. The processional screech of chairs gave away their eager desire that it might be Anna finally arriving. Anna would give meaning to their being here and that was what they wanted more than anything now. An unmasking of all of this mystery.

II

The ninth and final guest looked and sounded like a policeman. He had the formally reserved disposition of a cop they agreed.

"You wouldn't happen to be Terry, would you?" They all laughed when Terry made it obvious he didn't get the joke.

Dennis held up the card marking Terry's place at the table. "Elementary, my dear Watson."

"Inviting all your exes to a party, she's nuts," Grace said.

Grace started laughing uproariously again, setting them all off.

Terry, as taciturn as Jack on first acquaintance, didn't join in the laughter. He was usually a good looking forty but now he looked tired and withdrawn. Looking and no doubt feeling much older, his life unsociable and difficult since Anna had left him so suddenly. Being a mechanic and not a policeman, Terry was unimpressed with the jolting movement of the cable car and would not join them at the dinner table because he wanted to lie down.

"Look, I've come a long way, so if one of you could show me to my room, I would be grateful."

"We have no rooms as such," Patrick answered. "At least not yet."

Terry growled "nonsense" or something to that effect as he put his mobile to his ear.

"And you can't call or text from here, I'm afraid?" Patrick said.

"What do you mean?" Terry said. "We're on a mountain."

"Well, we've all tried several times over," Dennis replied patiently. "Patrick's theory is that being situated between two peaks means that transmission is nigh on impossible."

Terry ended up lying on the living room sofa. Patrick recognised a clear case of vertigo when he saw one. Terry had looked as white as the snow outside when he'd got out of the cable car, his feet and hands shaking. Too macho to admit it to a room of strangers.

It was getting dark outside.

And still no sign of Anna.

Chapter Four

I

They were all admiring a large black and white canvas photo of Anna laughing at a party, resting over the fireplace. Her hands clasping her thighs as she bent over in hysterics, her huge brown eyes conveying the ecstasy of her pure joy to the viewer. It dominated the room no matter where you sat.

"Putting the name cards out was Anna's way of letting us all know that none of us is him," Simon said.

"What do we know about him?" Grace said.

The room went silent.

"Not a hell of a lot," Patrick said. "I mean, nobody's ever seen him face-to-face."

"Who the hell is this guy, the friggin' boogeyman?" Jack asked, laughing at them. "That's how you're acting."

"Seems like it, doesn't it?" Simon said.

"Or maybe," Dennis said, arriving with coffees and brandies, "he just wants us to think that."

"What do you mean?" Jeff said, his eyes narrowing.

"Well," Dennis said defensively. "I mean, if you look at the greatest serial killers in history, they look so ordinary." He smiled putting an Irish coffee in front of dozing Grace and handing Jeff his Jack Daniels and Coke. "Like you and me."

"Speak for yourself," Jack said.

"I'll know him when he arrives," Jeff said, knocking back the Jack Daniel's whisky and gasping with satisfaction. "And he's going to wish he hadn't."

"We'll leave him to you then, Jeff," Jack replied, pouring more whisky into Grace's coffee at her request. Everyone except Jeff couldn't help but laugh, even the photographed Anna hanging on the wall appeared to smile that little bit wider.

II

They embarked on a tour of the west wing of the house ending in a glass-roofed Victorian conservatory larger and lighter than the living room and containing by far the most interesting feature as its centrepiece: a life-sized statue of Anna. A statue capturing all of her nude beauty magnificently in its carefully chiselled worship. There was not an excess gram of fat to be found on her immaculate, model-gorgeous frame.

Anna, ever the dedicated party girl, owed more to gifted genetics than the puritan dedication of honed exercise and strict diet, and all were thrust back for a moment into a once glorious past they'd shared with this body. It was the reason, though only Jack was readily willing to admit it to himself, why they'd made this monumental journey to the Tyrol.

"It's hideous," Simon said.

Grace agreed that it was a "ghastly" thing.

Jack, the first to leave, was the only one uninterested in it, perhaps because he was the only one who'd regularly looked on bodies like this and touched them intimately since Anna.

The sculptor did not entirely like Anna. There was an egotistical mocking quality to it, an undertone that did not meet the appraising eye pleasantly.

The naughty grin playing out on Anna's youthful features spoke of the iconic expression of Marilyn Monroe stepping out onto the sidewalk grate while attempting to hold onto her billowing skirt, of those achingly attractive women touched with that other light. The manufactured smirk, not Anna's. At least not all of Anna. The unnatural life in the expression would keep some of them up half the night, though they knew not why.

III

Jeff was the only one who slept through to 3 am. 3 am marked the long-overdue arrival of Anna.

The rooms were named after colours but were not decorated as such. This was another mystery to all but Dennis. Dennis, as usual, retreated to academia and fiction, referring to Poe's *Masque of the Red Death* and Prince Prospero's directions for his palace. Shirley Jackson's Hill House also abided to this colour coordinated convention. Jackson's *The Haunting Of Hill House* one of Anna's favourite novels, Dennis recalled.

Dennis was allocated the red room and sat up reading half the night. Grace the purple room in which she found the mattress too soft and ill-defined to relax into sleep. Jack started to unwind in the green room, listening to hip-hop on his iPod, his dozing turning to full sleep minutes later. Tony in the yellow room remained wide-eyed with the beginnings of the grogginess of a hangover. The alcohol was letting the demons in rather than letting them out, and that statue of Anna Tony could not fully exorcise from his troubled mind.

IV

The corridor ended as Tony found yet another strangely familiar room. Another room with high ceilings and wide-open spaces too vast to light or heat sufficiently.

There was firewood in the fireplace.

Firewood and an axe.

Now Tony had located the axe, he immediately broke into a run. He knew where he was headed this time. He was heading for Anna.

V

The at first faint and then increasingly more urgent banging at five after three in the morning got them all to leave their rooms and gather in the corridor. All except Jack, who was lost to the hip rhythmic in-your-face attitude of Kanye West on his iPod and a forever leaping Mario on his Nintendo Switch. Someone was having some kind of a fit downstairs, Jack decided, eventually taking out his earphones.

Someone attacking the walls downstairs with a sledgehammer it sounded like to Grace. It didn't take long for them to realise that it was coming from the conservatory. There were no walls in the conservatory.

Patrick was the first on the scene to witness the dark, ghostly figure swinging the fire-wood axe at the statue of Anna, attempting to destroy its features in wider and wilder arcs with each swing. He sought to obliterate Anna's statue into the misshapen, disfigured wreck that was his memory of her.

"Put it down," Dennis said.

Patrick and Dennis considered stopping Tony, taking advancing steps but thought better of it when the dark figure spun around, axe poised to strike. Instead, Patrick merely requested that the silhouetted figure, a figure he now recognised to be a severely drunk and broken Tony, stop doing this to himself. The others huddled in the doorway in dressing gowns and robes.

VI

They were all deeply shocked by what they saw in Tony's expression.

64

His eyes wide and wild, Tony squinted with sudden vulnerability at the invasion of light, administering a final swing before he was stopped by sheer weight of numbers and dragged away from the broken statue.

"You don't understand!" Tony said desperately. "I'm trying to save her."

Tony wailed, his crying possessing deep soulful suffering that touched everyone in the room. "Save her," he repeated faintly.

They consoled him before the statue made a final creaking noise as its head rolled onto the floor, resting at their feet. It confirmed what the lower indentations he'd made had suggested.

"Oh my God!" Grace screamed, the others gasped or turned their heads. A combination of terror and nausea hit them all at once.

"God no!" Dennis cried out.

The neck of the statue revealed a spinal cord jutting out of the decapitated cross-section of the neck and ending in the now very real severed head in front of them. The head propped unevenly on its side by the stub of Anna's spinal cord.

Anna had finally arrived.

VII

Tony ran into the night, uncaring of the lack of light and the steepness of the drop, not caring that his unpacked luggage was still in the house, or that he was not suitably dressed for the wind chill factor as he sprinted down towards the cable car on the north-eastern side of the house. Before the rest of them had attired the necessary clothing to pursue, Tony was inside the cable car and on his way down.

It was warmer inside the cable car but he was still shivering. The car slid down about five feet before there was a tortured shriek as the car stopped, bobbing like a yo-yo for a moment. The car started swinging in the night and teetering over the unfathomable precipice below.

Just swinging there, swinging for a long second that took the breath from its stunned and horrified audience.

Terry, his mechanic's mind working overtime, was the first to look up at the almost severed cable. A cable that would shortly give way. Nothing could stop that now, Terry saw.

"We have to get to him," Patrick said.

"There's no way," Terry said.

Another screech of metal and a rumble like a cruise ship going down into a cold cruel sea and the decision was taken out of their hands. The car swung for the last time and dropped straight down, crashing against the jagged mountainside and out of view. It had nearly nine hundred more feet to fall in the darkness.

A darkness that could only be certain death for Tony.

VIII

Patrick shut the iron-studded oak door on the bitter chill wind with a clang, slumping his back against it. There was defeat in his body language. Terry put a hand on his shoulder. "All right?"

Patrick nodded, "I'm fine."

Terry patted him on the shoulder in consolation.

"Tony was in shock. I don't think he even knew what he was doing," Ronnie interrupted, his voice uneven.

"Well, one of us did," Dennis replied, voicing aloud what they all secretly suspected. "Know, I mean."

"What're you talking about?" Jeff said.

"Somebody cut that cable, that's what he means," Grace said, hearing the rise of hysteria in her voice.

"Why would they do that?" Jack said, looking as confused as Jeff standing next to him.

"Why do you think?" Grace said, "One of you's him!"

Chapter Five

I

Everyone's hysterics over, Patrick, the voice of sanity, attempted to put tonight's unfolding events into perspective as he clinically dissected the motivation behind their invites as they sipped their brandies and coffees by the lit inglenook fireplace. Eyes were darting back and forth, the room heavy with suspicion. Trying to work out who had the opportunity and inclination to have booby-trapped the cable car, who amongst them capable of murder.

Each of them established in their minds who they could confide in, who they could forge an alliance with to ensure survival. With so much going on mentally they were all only half listening to Patrick's theorising. There was a homicidal maniac on the loose, perhaps standing right next to them.

II

"We can't delay any longer," Patrick said. "We should make an SOS call."

"That's not an option," Dennis replied.

"What do you mean?"

"Come see for yourself."

Dennis and Patrick descended a long dark hallway ending in a small study not much bigger than a booth. It was the communications room.

"See," Dennis said.

The CB radio was smashed up along with the Morse code kit. Everything of use in the small grey room ransacked and vandalised.

"Surely someone will realise that we're stranded up here without means of communication?" Patrick said.

"Not necessarily. Here." Dennis grabbed a book on the table and handed it to Patrick. "Look at the logbook."

"This can't be right." Patrick leafed through the pages until he found the point where the biro writing stopped and flipped back through the logged entries again as though he doubted what he had read. "There hasn't been an entry made in nearly eighteen months."

Dennis nodded glumly.

Patrick sprung into life, frantically rifling through cupboards and then the desk drawers.

"What's the matter? What're you looking for?"

"I was in here earlier," Patrick confessed, stopping his searching to look Dennis in the eye. "There was a flare gun. I saw it myself."

"Not anymore."

III

"Are we sure this isn't some kind of a *joke*?" Simon got up out of his seat to address the group. "Ronnie and I have been discussing it."

Ronnie gave the others a weary look that said: "leave me out of it."

It was 3:26 am and their eyes were heavy and red-rimmed. None of them wanted to deal with it at this stage. It was etched on their haggard, defeated faces. Patrick and Dennis returned to the open planned sitting area large enough to be a lobby. They'd returned from the communications room not speaking to one another and looking jaded.

"You think this is a joke?" Grace said.

"Not so much a joke as an elaborate hoax," Simon responded, looking around for support. "It would be just like Anna, wouldn't it? When you stop for a moment and consider our predicament."

Patrick shook his head as he took a seat next to Grace. "Anna wouldn't joke about something like this."

"How do you know that though?" Simon said.

"Because she's not fucked in the head," Jack said, not even bothering to look up from his Nintendo Switch video game.

"Well," Simon smiled, "it'll all seem less fucked in the head when she walks in arm in arm with Tony laughing her ass off at all of you!"

Jack looked up momentarily from his calculated button bashing. He was about to answer but decided at the last moment to bite his words. Where the others had a conversation as a way of dealing with what they'd witnessed Jack immersed himself in his private world of death as escapism. He was playing *Streetfighter V* as Ryu, using fireballs to set traps and when his computer opponent leapt over them, he slammed them mercilessly with Ryu's trademark dragon punch.

"Well, I'm not fucking in on it," Jeff scoffed. "I came to start a new life with Anna."

"Nor me," Terry said.

Grace left the room momentarily. She was dressed only in a long T-shirt as a makeshift nightgown. Jeff's eyes along with Dennis' instantly held on the backs of her smooth shapely thighs for a long second.

Patrick was only looking at Simon, concern still pinched on the brow of his high forehead. "You remember what you spoke to me about Simon? What happened to your friend on stage?" Patrick said with a degree of secrecy and confidentiality. "And how you reacted to death then – carrying on in the role?"

There was a glint of recognition in Jeff's eye as Patrick said this, and he nodded to himself.

"This is different," Simon responded.

Grace emerged with a tall glass of water which she put next to Simon along with two capsules which he ignored. Grace looked intently at him but spoke as kindly as she could manage.

"Look, you're in shock. It's perfectly understandable. But you have to accept one thing. I'm a doctor." Grace was talking very carefully, pointing to the door, "And that's Anna's body out there."

Simon let out a high-pitched sound that was not quite a laugh and buried his head in his hands so that only the egg-shaped dome of his head was visible.

It took them all a moment to realise that he was crying.

"Oh, God!" Simon sobbed. "She's gone, isn't she?"

"Yes," Patrick replied for them all, patting Simon's back with light and awkward affection. "I'm afraid she is."

Chapter Six

I

"We fulfil a need," Patrick swept a hand around the room of his audience, the other in his jacket pocket. "All this fulfils a need for him."

A laughing Anna provided a backdrop over the fireplace, her eyes alive with joy. Patrick didn't want to look at her. He wasn't the only one.

"And what need would that be?" Jeff said, providing the voice of scepticism as he crossed his arms. "What are a madman's needs exactly?"

There was an accusatory undercurrent in every statement now.

"He wants to find out everything about Anna," Patrick said, addressing them all as if he were in a seminar. "He's completely obsessed about her."

"No shit," Jack said.

"Let him go on," Dennis said, settling down on the sofa with a G&T. "Any kind of insight at this stage is going to be useful." Dennis nodded to Patrick. "You were saying."

Patrick continued. "His needs are to unravel and destroy every part of her being. It torments him still." Seeing they still weren't convinced, Patrick added, "You see, he can't form normal relationships since Anna so he does this instead."

Patrick took a sip of his drink. He needed it. "He's playing a game in which we're the trophies. It's the only way he can go on living."

"Trophies?" Jeff again, the scepticism still in his voice.

"Yes. We're a prize," Ronnie said shakily. "You see, he wants to find out which of us had the most fulfilling, intimate relationship with Anna."

Dennis bluntly said straight out what Patrick was working up to, "And therefore the most satisfying kill."

"Surely he doesn't expect to kill all of us?" Grace said.

They all let that hang in the air for a moment as a stunned hush was observed throughout the living room. A room which seemed suddenly that much smaller in this silence. This deathly silence.

II

"All I'm saying is," Jack said, getting up off the sofa, looking around for support, "I think we should each be armed with a knife tonight."

"Nobody's going to be armed," Grace said forcibly. "If we're armed somebody will be killed, either accidentally or intentionally. Can't you see that?"

"Yeah," Jack responded. "But we'll all have the same chance that way."

"Forget it," Dennis said. "Nobody else is going to die."

"He's right," Ronnie said.

"Of course he's right," Grace replied.

"You're all in denial," Jack said. "Right, Patrick?"

Jeff put his hands on his hips. "Well, what're we going to do?"

"There's nothing more we can do tonight," Simon said. "Let's sleep on it and decide in the morning."

"I agree," Patrick said, speaking for the majority again. "We should all just go to our rooms and lock ourselves in. The storm will probably be gone by morning."

"You're forgetting one thing," Jack said.

"And what's that?" Patrick said.

"Not all of us have locks on our doors."

The debates started up again.

III

No one wanted to leave the group and its safety in numbers for their beds until they'd rationalised what they'd witnessed less than an hour ago. With daybreak and a fully lit house three hours away, they wanted answers. And so, the debates went on, as they slowly worked their way back to the subject of their mysterious host.

The psychiatrist's musing had only served to raise the paranoia a few notches. The idea that they were living and breathing some psychopath's fantasy, completely cut-off from the rest of the world, gripped them in its sobering thought.

"He wants us to feel truly alone," Patrick summed up. "Truly isolated as he has been. Anna never really loved him."

Patrick recognised that his audience wasn't looking at him but at each other. The looks they exchanged were ugly and calculating. Fear, self-preservation and ruthlessness the dominating emotions.

"Nice try," Jeff said, shaking his head, referring to Patrick's half-hearted attempt to goad the ego of the killer into a reaction. "Think you'll have to do just a little bit better than that though."

They all, slowly but surely, departed in twos and threes. Grace, Patrick and Dennis represented the academic tribal group. Simon and Jack the suddenly abandoned couple. Terry, Jeff and Ronnie the remaining tribe of commonality.

Setting up their alliances, their pacts and their respective game plans for survival. Traps to be set, suspicions to be aired. It was far from a game though, and yet, it felt more than ever like they were playing one.

The long licks of the fire finally went out, but there was no one left in the living room to attend to it. Somewhere in the house, somebody was plotting whilst happily playing along with all this.

IV

Imagination had quickly become reality until reality was overtaken by pressing madness. Cabin fever was the clinical term. Patrick's term, but what it felt like to be cooped up in this house was beyond definition.

Subsequently, the killer's confidence was growing by the minute and they sensed he was no longer content to just watch. Someone else would have to die tonight in this game of elimination to justify this confidence.

V

Dennis was still up, sat drinking spirits in the living room, and raising a toast to an onlooking Anna smiling away in black and white. He ordinarily wrote at this time. The quiet darkness at night brought an edge to his work he'd always thought. Revelations in thought came and left Dennis with each glass that passed his lips.

Perhaps there was both a cold-hearted murderer and a crazy defending himself by killing first. Perhaps.

That had been the case in one of his books. He'd brought the ex alive in it on the page and now here he was mirroring it. He wouldn't tell the others though, not until the suspicions died down.

That book was one of his best sellers and for the life of him he couldn't remember the title, that's how soused he was. The original Raymond Chandler.

"Can't sleep?" a masculine voice asked, startling Dennis.

"Jesus," Dennis patted his heart.

Patrick, in his dressing-gown, admitted he could not sleep either.

"I find walking does the trick for me," Patrick smiled "Ten minutes and I'm out like a light."

"Perhaps not tonight though."

"Perhaps not tonight," Patrick admitted.

"Why don't you join me then?" Dennis asked, nodding to the whisky decanter and the almost full bottle of *Gordon's* G&T in front of him on the coffee table.

"I guarantee this will put you out like a light."

Patrick, shaking his head at Dennis' offer of a nightcap, bid him goodnight, and Dennis was eager to accompany the others wherever they may be. He could hear someone was playing billiards in the games room.

"Safety in numbers," Dennis said to himself sensibly as he drained some more of the penultimate bottle of *Gordon's* G&T left in the house. Dennis followed Patrick into the corridor where he was nowhere to be seen. His ghostlike disappearance was unsettling to Dennis.

Had he imagined the whole episode? He was losing it, but at this point, none of them could have been said to be completely sane.

All of them were potential killers.

VI

"Your break," Terry said.

The hollow clatter of billiard balls colliding filled the games room.

"Don't know what it is," Terry said. "Just feels like I can trust you."

"Same here," Jeff admitted.

Jeff and Terry, united under the camaraderie of being the only two East-end born and bred boys far from home, continued to play Pool in the games room. They were acting as if it were their local, and the beer they sipped not foreign and oversweet and left out in the snow to cool.

The six-packs of Fosters and Budweiser had quickly gone leaving them with supplies of Austrian beer only. The Gosser beer that Terry and Jeff were just getting used to had been in small supply and had now gone. They were left with bottle after bottle of regional beer and were making the best of it. There were two types Anna had stocked in her cellar, Falkenstein and Mohrenbrau. Both Terry and Jeff marginally preferred the Falkenstein – the lesser of two evils – which they referred to as "another Frankenstein, mate?" or "pass me some more Frankenstein, will you?" which cracked them both up. The joke being that only Frankenstein would drink this shit, oiling his neck bolts with it.

Jeff, suddenly serious, looked Terry in the eye. "You know what I'm getting at. This whole set up's wrong."

Terry nodded agreement but gave Jeff a look to say that he would not approach this disturbing subject yet, not until he had more beer inside him and more games of Pool under his belt. He was enjoying the escapism too much. His mind needed it like his throat needed the cool beer.

That was the comforting atmosphere of familiarity they were hoping to create with their alliance here tonight. Taking them away from the horror of their situation so that they could think straight and work out who among them was the ex. Both were leading up to their chief suspect, but all in good time.

"Can't help feeling there's something I'm missing," Terry looked around the room at the numerous pictures of Anna. "Something obvious."

The Pool table was a six-by-three affair with the coin-up disabled. The cloth was green baize, brand new like the rest of the furnishings, and the balls were the straightforward English version of seven red balls, seven yellow balls with a black eight ball. Jeff was currently playing yellows, and at the table, three balls up. Edging an easy cut to the generously sized middle pocket that Terry had speculated was perhaps as much as an inch too wide to be regulation. It was at that moment that they got down to what had been left unsaid.

"You know," Terry stroked his chin. "Most of the people here suspect me because they figure the cable car was booby-trapped and muggins here is the mechanic."

"They're scared, that's all. They won't do anything about it," Jeff said, snookering Terry when he saw the yellow on the top cushion could not be cut or doubled with any certainty.

"How much expertise do you think you need to sever a bloody cable?" Terry was still pleading his case as he successfully got out of Jeff's snooker with a pretty handy two cushion escape, but leaving Jeff on again nevertheless.

"Distancing yourself from the others gave you the opportunity though," Jeff said.

"You don't think that..."

Jeff shrugged. "Just looking at it from their point of view."

"I was knackered," Terry said defensively. "I wanted to lie down, that's all."

Jeff chalked his cue to satisfaction, cued carefully, and looked up at the ball over the pocket at the opposite end of the table. His forehead furrowed in a wave of neat lines and ripples.

80

"Don't let it worry you," Jeff said. "I'll be the one around here calling the shots soon." He saw the reflection of his smile in the shiny newness of the balls. "And I've got a plan of my own."

VII

Ronnie couldn't sleep. His legs were as restless as his mind as he contemplated moving the dresser away from his door and stepping out into the darkness of the corridor to see if someone was lurking outside as the noises had suggested for the last hour.

Ronnie also thought about calling a meeting and telling the others about what he'd discovered in the cellar.

VIII

Jeff dispatched the two remaining yellows with ease but miscued badly on the black, blaming it on the cue-tip being too new and thin and not properly broken in yet.

Terry wasn't playing his shot, an edgy look on his face. Something was getting to him again. Something he was building up to like this shot.

"Why are you here, exactly?" Terry said.

"Me?" Jeff paused to neck some more ice cool beer. He gasped at the refreshment it gave him. "Hard to say really. I went with Anna for going on five months before she took off. It was the best five months of my otherwise miserable life." Jeff laughed. "When you put it like that I suppose –"

"For me, it was just the sex."

They both laughed.

Terry agreed that Anna had indeed been special. Special enough to make this trip. Their conversation soon reverted to playing detective in between some half-decent Pool.

Jeff spoke again after he settled his nerves to cut the black in the centre pocket after Terry had missed a double.

"You probably won't believe this, but I was going to get married. At least I was until Anna contacted me."

In the next game, after pocketing off the break, Jeff missed a cut he assumed full enough to be a formality. Returning to the table after Terry missed his pot, Jeff pocketed six balls in a row. Terry caught up on balls pocketed at his next visit as he relaxed his cueing arm and sank seven reds in a row. He contemplated a tall shot on the black he doubted he could make, adding more chalk for confidence.

"Married?" Terry said. "Didn't have you down as the marrying type."

"Yeah, this weekend. Last weekend was my stag-do, if you can believe it," Jeff grinned. "All this has proved a bit more exciting."

Terry didn't smile.

"I'm joking, Terry."

"Oh."

Terry made the rail shot, surprising himself more than Jeff's marital revelation.

"Nice shot. Up for another?"

"Sure."

Jeff pulled the disabled coin-op release, causing a rattle of balls for a new game, not caring if he woke the rest of the house or not.

Terry looked up at a large black and white photo of Anna smoking in a cafe. It didn't seem like a real cafe, rather an artist's impression of what one should look like. Anna's eyes were deep dark pools that drew you in.

"She was something, wasn't she?"

"She was," Jeff agreed.

"You think he killed her first or drugged her and let her suffocate in all that clay, cement or whatever nasty shit that statue is made of?"

"Dunno. This may sound callous but now's she dead, I don't care. It's kind of a relief."

They both looked at the huge black and white photo. A past love in freeze-frame.

Terry sighed. "I know what you mean. You feel you can move on with your life. Knowing she's gone."

Terry smiled at the ridiculousness of what he'd said considering their predicament. They were stranded up here. Perhaps not for long if the killer was as good as he boasted to be.

"Only it took me coming all this way to discover that," Terry said.

"Not me."

Terry arched his eyebrows. "What do mean, not you?"

"Put it this way. I've got enough problems in my life to keep me alive."

"At least now you've got a buddy looking out for you."

Jeff paused to look up from his shot for a moment, contemplating what Terry had said.

IX

Jack stuffed his designer shirts into his Adidas rucksack. There was a way out of this. All he needed was the guts to go through with it.

Chapter Seven

I

"As I say," Terry took another sip of his beer. "At least now you've got a buddy looking out for you."

"Is that what this is?" Jeff said.

Jeff studied Terry, unsure if he could believe this, but nodded after a time. He was a betting man by nature, and Terry was from his cultural backyard. Their friendship already a natural fit. He'd stand more of a chance if he trusted Terry.

Terry was keen to change the subject, nodding to the Chelsea FC tattoo peering under the sleeve of Jeff's chocolate brown Lambretta T-shirt. Terry was a die-hard Hammers fan. Jeff laughed at Terry's gripe at Chelsea nabbing West Ham's best young players in recent times.

Jeff broke explosively, scattering the balls with a satisfying thwack that sent reds and yellows crashing against the cushions and a ball of each colour into the bottom corner and side pockets respectively.

"You go to any of the games?"

"Season ticket holder," Jeff boasted, unable to keep the pride out of his voice as he carefully considered which balls were in the more potable position and which to leave. Leaping ahead four or five possible shots in his mind.

Jeff settled on the reds after eyeing up the three reds which cut to his favoured centre pocket being too much for him to resist. Hours of practice as a kid cutting the blue into the centre pocket on a snooker table, watching the blue deflect in an unnaturally straight path and dropping in the pocket thousands of times over, made this type of shot a formality.

Terry whistled at Jeff's season ticket boast. "How much did that set you back?"

"Too much."

"Good seats?"

"I don't sit next to Abramovich if that's what you mean."

Terry didn't smile. He was moving towards voicing his suspicion. Yeah, he'd voice it. See what Jeff made of his little theory.

"Listen, what do you make of that writer guy…as an accomplice, I mean?"

"Dennis the menace? Not a chance." Jeff shook his head. "No, you're way off there."

"Why not?"

"Too fat, too lazy, too bookish."

"Have you read any of his books? Apparently, they're all cunning murder mysteries."

"My sister used to be a proof-reader for Penguin. She's an agent now, and she reads him. His plots are so fantastic she doesn't care who's done it by the end of the book. He's not very perceptive in observing human nature either. His lead character – Dawkins or Dawlish, I can never remember which – is a boring old fart who speculates about every little unimportant thing before pulling the killer's motive way out of left field."

"Wouldn't this scenario be deemed fantastic?"

"Yeah, but the guy's got no flare," Jeff said as if Dennis Harker's questionable narrative skills were a logical indication of his unlikelihood of him being a murderer.

"He's got brains, but not the sharp tactical nous to set up something like this." Jeff smiled. "He's a gin and tonic drinker, for Christ's sake."

When Terry didn't laugh, Jeff said: "Trust me, good old Dennis-the-menace ain't the deranged ex. No chance. He knows nothing about what goes through a killer's mind other than the obvious."

"And you do?" Terry's eyes narrowed.

Jeff's gaze became intense, finding Terry's own staring back at him confrontationally.

"I'm not the one everyone suspects, remember," Terry momentarily dropped his eyes. "You'd do well to remember that."

"Just speculating," Terry said defensively.

Jeff played his next pot nicely. He studied the table and not Terry, his voice cold. "So was I, mate."

Jeff's accusing look was gone by the time he played his next shot. He made a mess of a tricky cut and cursed himself for taking it on when he missed the jaws by a good inch, not even rattling them. Terry also overcut his ball, an even easier pot, to the same troublesome pocket.

Neither particularly cared. Not with the conversation they were currently having.

"What about the bald guy?" Terry said.

"That's more like it. Now you're thinking like me. Haven't stopped thinking about him. You're not the theatre-going type, are you Terry?"

Terry laughed unexpectedly. "And you are?"

"Occasionally. He's an actor, you know. And he's not bald. Not normally anyway."

"An actor? Am I the only one around here not famous or something?"

Jeff didn't laugh as he took a swig of ice-cool Falkenstein beer.

"You're not exactly Mister current affairs, are you? Get this, the geezer has a skinhead for a very good reason."

"Go on."

"Good old jolly-hockey-sticks-Simon's a suspect in a murder investigation. That Johnny guy from Eastenders. You know, the one who was having an affair with his mother-in-law. That Lisa."

"Don't watch it." Recognition passed over Terry's eyes. "Oh, I know who you mean. No, that's not him."

"Thought you said you didn't watch it? I know that's not him, you plonker. He was poisoned last week, for real."

"No shit?"

"No shit."

Jeff let this sink in for a moment. "And dear old Simon's a suspect."

Terry didn't care about their Pool game now, setting his cue down to give this his full attention.

"You know what?" Terry said. "I didn't buy that sobbing act either. He looks a sneaky cunt to me."

Jeff nodded meaningfully. "Personally, that's where my money would be."

II

Jack sat watching the spear of light under his door, his packed rucksack on the floor next to him as it had been for the last half hour. His room had no lock on the door.

If someone was lingering outside, the light beneath the door would break and act as a warning device before the unlocked door was opened.

In the semi-darkness, Jack completed his final push-up in a slow controlled two-second up - two-second down prolonging of his form. His veiny tattooed arms bunched and bulged, preparing his body for what he had to do.

Never taking his eye off the bar of light under the door, Jack felt an endorphin-induced calm overcoming adrenalin in his system. He was fully warmed up, stretched, pumped and ready for action.

Now was the time to go.

The rock-climbing gear they'd found in the equipment shed he'd lied about when he'd told the rest of them it was quite useless in his opinion. For him only, it was an escape route out of this nightmare. Somebody with his qualifications, training and physical conditioning could make the descent.

The others had to help themselves.

III

Simon's eyes were shut, as he sat in the lotus position on his bed, attempting to relax and clarify his thoughts.

It was a little after 5 am and he had no intention of sleeping. He could hear the distant rattle of Pool balls going around the table as they were potted on a fairly regular basis. Someone was playing pool to take their mind off of the dreadful events that had unfolded earlier.

Odd! Very odd.

Or perhaps one of them was the relaxing guilty party? He refocused. Simon was trying to get a feel for this guy. All the endless speculating was a pointless exercise for him. Aligning his professional acting instincts of what would motivate a killer would reveal the guilty party. That's what Simon had to stick to. How he would think, what he'd be doing tonight.

Playing Pool either alone or with another guest did not fit the killer's profile. He'd be waiting out an opportunity, deciding with careful calculation the risks of such an attack. After all, with them cut off from the world he had all the time he needed to line up his next prey. With one person dead, he was sure that the killer would want to strike while the guests were paralysed with fear. That's what his instincts told him.

They'd be two fewer guests instead of one in the morning, of that he was certain. Three deaths including Anna. Locking himself in his room prevented him from being the next victim.

He replayed in his mind every erudite word he'd stored from what the psychiatrist had given them all as a prognosis of this killer's state of mind. Would he be jealous of the success of someone like him, or would he fear Dennis' insight? Would he hate Patrick for knowing far more about Anna's emotional needs, or that Grace, being a woman, and a medical doctor, would probably be better at satisfying Anna sexually?

He felt a sudden adrenalin-fed surge of jealousy himself at the thought. He too wanted Anna for himself.

But all this was mere speculation. He needed substance. He needed to be sure.

Simon got up to check the dresser he'd dragged in front of his bedroom door was securely in place. He wouldn't risk leaving this room tonight, it was far too precarious in light of what he knew. Simon finally felt tired enough to get some needed rest.

The rattling Pool ball noises ceased but the games had only just begun. Shortly somebody was going to die and there would be one less person to suspect. Simon was certain of it.

IV

Grace took a shower in the compact en-suite, propping a chair up against the door. She felt she was being watched, even now.

Grace's frayed nerves confused the beating of the shower's spray with approaching footsteps. Grace tried not to think of Janet Leigh and Psycho as she soaped herself in record time, the hot water bleeding down her body. She stood naked in front of the bathroom mirror, cut off at the hip like the skilful censorship of a movie camera. Grace did not know if she was trembling from being cold, frightened, or most disturbing of all, quivering from a perverse growing excitement.

Sex and death were said to be closer akin than we could ever comfortably admit to ourselves. She'd have to ask Patrick about that when the moment was right. She wondered, completely unsuspecting of the psychiatrist as the potential killer, what he'd be doing tonight to try and flush out their mysterious quarry.

The ex only made her think of Anna, though. She'd been so full of life... alive in that statue. How awful to see her again, for the last time, like that.

With this thought, Grace took the gleaming steak knife she'd taken from the kitchen earlier from its concealment under the towel by the sink. She, unlike Janet Leigh, had been holding the knife while in the shower.

That knife ended up under her pillow. Easily in reach, if she felt hands on her neck during the night.

Grace found she was still too wound up to sleep. It was gone 5 am, she knew this only from her internal body clock. It was past 6 am when her mind finally surrendered into smothering darkness.

Only the guilty slept easily tonight.

V

Such a descent required the strength to comfortably hold your body weight for long periods. No one else here, Jack thought, capable of this.

That's how Jack justified this decision to himself. Self-preservation made it no decision at all. Any one of them could be the killer.

He carried out an equipment check. The hiking boots he'd nicked from a sleeping Dennis would have to do in place of the desired rock shoes.

Jack had to laugh at his stealing them from right under Dennis' nose. The writer was the only one he hadn't suspected or feared to be the killer. He was fat, slow-witted and for a writer not even perceptive.

He'd been content to just let conversations pass him by, coming in now and again with his unfunny one-liners. Famous people weren't especially smart, they were only driven.

Jack had crept into his room and stolen the hiking boots without a hint of fear, putting the soles to his socks. They were a ten, he was a nine, or a nine and a half. Like the rest of the equipment, it was a close enough fit.

There was no helmet or protection gear as such. What Jack did have was a weathered Kernmantel fifty metre rope, well-worn but looking strong and dynamic. Its thickness of eleven millimetres substantial enough to be able to support his eighty-seven-kilo weight.

The rusty bolts, belay devices and karabiners were a bit old-school but would hold. The harness looked as though it had seen better days, but again would do the job.

All in all, there was enough useable equipment here to entice him into making the descent.

The flashlight was a bonus; he'd found it in Tony's abandoned rucksack (which Tony wouldn't be needing any more) on the porch. He also found a pack of twenty Benson and Hedges cigarettes in Tony's drawer which he stuffed gratefully into his pocket.

It was risky, but Jack fancied his chances more with this makeshift equipment and the elements than surviving another night here. He still had no idea who was behind this. Aside from Dennis, and possibly Ronnie, it could be any one of them. That was the other deciding factor in his decision to leave tonight.

He'd examined the rock face earlier in the dying light, the last variable that could make or break his plans. It possessed neither the saltiness nor the erosion he feared he'd find. The bolts could not pop out due to corroding, crumbling rock and leave him falling God knows how far in the unfathomable darkness.

Jack crept in his socks, out into the corridor with his equipment on his back. The thick hallway carpet absorbing any floorboard creaks the extra weight of the climbing equipment might have made.

When a door opened to his right, Jack dropped to his knees, hiding behind a stairwell bannister.

Jack waited a few more seconds before deciding they were not going his way. Whoever it was had taken the corridor leading to the conservatory and that hideous entombment of the only woman he'd ever loved. The woman he would never hold in his arms again.

Jack gritted his teeth. Soon he'd be out of this house of horrors.

On the stairs, Jack sensed someone behind him. A glance told him there was no one there. His other niggling senses continued to tell him otherwise, but this childlike fear he put down to nerves messing with his mind.

When he'd reached the porch, Jack put the hiking boots on. The rope hoisted on his shoulder, his Adidas rucksack on his back, Jack was all set to go. Jack took a deep breath and ploughed through the heavy snow. It was an energy-sapping fifty-yard journey to the mountain's edge.

The wind-chill had picked up enough to make it uncomfortable, and he had to steel himself to concentrate. He'd be shielded from it once he started his descent, he told himself.

Jack descended expertly for about thirty feet before stopping.

"What the –"

Jack felt his foot meet an opening. He lowered himself to reveal that it was a long man-made shaft that went on further than the light of his torch could probe. There were other shafts ten yards to his right and his left, and three more below him. About half a dozen or so openings in all.

What were they for?

Who cared, he had to keep going before the swirling wind picked up.

It was at that moment Jack felt the bolt strike his ear, hearing the snaking rope and stake fall past him with a whipping sound. He held on desperately, his grip slipping as he heard evil laughter from one of the above shafts.

Jack's sports bag slipped off his shoulder and fell open, his clothes dropping like bricks.

The laughter grew louder, maniacal.

"Fuck you!" Jack screamed, holding on with the fingertips of his left hand.

This was greeted with further laughter.

Jack's grip weakening, he attempted to swing down into one of the shafts beneath him. "Please. Please, God. Please."

Jack extended his toes but his heavy boots were unable to grip the shaft in what proved a tricky manoeuvre.

He overcompensated, feeling a sickening slide as he overbalanced on his heels and slipped backwards. Jack screamed as his sliding hands were scorched, as he failed to get a grip on the rock face.

Jack came away from the rock face altogether, feeling his jacket flap wildly as he plummeted like a skydiver, and then nothing but a thudding black wall of oblivion seconds later.

The second murder had gone much the way as the first, with unchallenged ease.

VI

Dennis heard and felt the wind fully in his ears like a cool hairdryer.

And then Dennis was falling.

He struck the protruding section of a rock face with a sickening thud that crushed his spinal cord and neck on impact. Then it was just his corpse that fell the rest of the way, dead weight, for the remaining nine hundred feet, until finally arresting on a plateau of rock, snow and ice.

It was an eerie sensation looking at your corpse, floating out of your body, and it was in that moment Dennis realised he was only dreaming.

Dennis awoke surprised to still be alive, his breath heaving.

Sweaty, Dennis got up and looked in the bathroom mirror. He didn't recognise the expression on his face, other than that he was grinning.

Dennis awoke a second time into what we know as reality, only on this occasion it was simply waking from one nightmare world into another.

A killer was on the loose tonight.

Chapter Eight

I

He'd always been good with faces. So, where had he seen Jack before? Ronnie fished for specifics in his subconscious as he entered the small gym in the basement adjoining the Jacuzzi and sauna.

The gym was cramped even though he was its only user. Every corner of its meagre square footage utilised to the full, consisting of seven Cybex machines to cater for each of the major muscle groups in the body: quads, hamstrings, pecs, abs, upper back, triceps and shoulders. Accompanied by a stair-master and a Reebok spin cycle for cardio.

There was no Concept Two rowing machine he'd come to rely on, no free-weights beyond a stacked pyramid set of steel dumbbells weighing between five and twenty kilograms. There was also a single silver Swiss ball for core stability, which called *The Prisoner* to mind and the ridiculous image of Patrick McGoohan being chased and caught by the weird island sentinel like a piece of giant bubblegum.

He laughed. "Yeah, I'm the prisoner all right."

Ronnie warmed up on the Stairmaster for ten minutes and lengthened and shortened his muscles to exhaustion on the machines for a further fifteen. He couldn't get used to the machines, feeling that they gave you too much assisted-leverage and drastically reduced the range of motion in each lift, and he failed to get a satisfying contraction of the muscles he wanted to isolate because of it. He didn't like the pec deck much either, it stressed and strained his chest in an unnatural way, and without a bench to perform dumbbell flys on he settled for a routine of old-school press-ups and dips on the stairs.

He stretched and cooled down on the Reebok spin cycle before stripping to his boxers and entering the sauna. The sauna took five minutes to warm up enough to make it worthwhile.

Ronnie had a 5kg dumbbell as a weapon, concealed under the gym towel he'd brought into the sauna with him. He was justified in doing so as he was being watched.

II

The sauna's ninety-five degrees of dry heat singed his nostrils, its sterilised scent recalling football changing rooms in his youth and muscle rub. Ronnie wondered if he'd done all the exercises in his *Men's Health* circuit. He'd done the best he could with the equipment available to him. Ronnie recalled where he'd seen Jack before. He'd subscribed to *Men's Health* magazine last Christmas and Jack had been a cover-model for *Men's Health* magazine a couple of months back, all smiles and washboard abs.

A personal trainer from Croydon, that was it. A trainer to some well-known actor preparing for his latest film role. Not this mysterious ex.

In his mind, he could see Jack smiling on the front cover.

Anna was also smiling at him beyond the grave in a pink bikini, a poster on the far gym wall from a photoshoot in an infinity pool.

That made three famous or semi-famous people in the house. Not surprising perhaps considering Anna's rare combination of keen intellect and exquisite beauty attracted numerous well-to-do suitors, high achievers and high-ranking professional people.

And then there was him, but he'd never quite got why Anna had taken to him in the first place. If he was looking at it from the others' point of view, he would have had himself as the first suspect on their list because of this obvious fact.

He was neither charming nor complicated.

It made little difference. He had Angela now and Anna was…

"Dead," he said quietly to himself. "Anna's dead."

Ronnie tried to shut his eyes like he always did in saunas to relax further. He found he couldn't close his eyes. He was weary of being shut in by the killer. The sauna temperature increased to its maximum, the tinted Perspex glass door shatterproof. Nightmares in this house could become reality at any moment and this had plagued him all night.

He'd been concerned about the murderer creeping up to him in the night and Ronnie was still worried about these breaths being his last. But he had to shut those thoughts out if he was to survive this, Ronnie reminded himself.

He trusted Jack. More so than any other person in this house. He'd approach Jack and sound him out. He had to confide in someone and Jack, he now thought, was that person.

As he bowed his head, a figure in a ski mask entered the gym and headed straight for Ronnie.

III

As the figure approached the sauna, he removed his ski mask and Ronnie saw that it was Terry. Along with Jeff and Patrick, Terry was Ronnie's chief suspect. Being the last to arrive and not present at dinner, no one had easier access to sabotaging that cable car than Terry.

Terry removed his jacket and ski pants and blew on his hands before entering the sauna.

"Morning. Any improvement in the weather?" Ronnie said amiably but considered leaving. He fumbled for his towel and the steel dumbbell concealed under it.

Terry kept his distance, sitting at the opposite end of the sauna on the top bench. Ronnie moved up to the top bench so that he could face Terry and not have his back to him.

"It's worse if anything," Terry said. "Don't count on any of us leaving here for days."

"See a way down?"

"Not unless you can fly."

Ronnie changed the subject. "You get much sleep?"

"Not much," Terry replied. "I necked two cans of Red Bull so that I didn't."

"Why?"

"Why do you think? So that nobody crept up on me in the night and slit my throat."

"There's a lock on your door though, isn't there?"

"Yeah, but there's such a thing as a skeleton key."

"So, you believe he'll try and kill again?" Ronnie said, deliberately trying to annoy Terry with naivety.

It worked.

"That's the whole point of us being here." Terry shook his head in disgust before exiting the sauna. "Who do you teach for a living, the fucking deaf and dumb?"

Ronnie's heart-rate monitor dropped fifteen beats a minute after Terry left. The sauna doing the trick as Ronnie's anxiety was shed as easily as the shiny film of sweat dripping onto the smooth pinewood bench.

His digital sports watch beeped that it was 8 am. It would be fully light by now. Perhaps the weather conditions were improving. He'd soon see.

A new man, he'd shower, shave and change before joining the others for breakfast.

Clear, rational thinking was what he needed if he was to see Angela again. Last night had been hard but he'd battled through the troubled sleep-deprivation.

The morning had brought a new resolve just as Ronnie told himself it would.

Yeah, Jack represented his best way out of this.

Perhaps his only chance.

Chapter Nine

I

The topic at breakfast was the sudden disappearance of Jack, which had immediately cast suspicion over everyone. Jack included.

Breakfast was set out as a team effort. An international buffet that you get with that all-you-can-eat hearty breakfast mentality in hotels and guesthouses across Europe: the generic no thrills cereals, cold meats and pastries. The essentials catering for everyone and no one.

Rationing had not begun yet, although it was suggested that they should start with the reality that they could be left stranded up here for some time in this brutal weather. The mysterious host had stocked the kitchen full of treats, though they were starting to suspect he'd stocked it only for himself. It would last weeks if the current killing rate was kept up. Nine guests to be fed had been reduced to only seven. Albeit with Jack only missing, but having searched everywhere they were willing to accept the worst.

II

Other than the house and equipment shed, there was only a small plot of acreage between the mountains and a sheer drop outside.

"Jack's not out here," Simon called out over the wind. "Let's head back."

"We can't just give up," Ronnie said,

"What's to give up? He's not out here."

Although only Ronnie seemed genuine in his regret of Jack's absence, the fearsome notion of his sudden disappearance touched all present. The second baffling murder had potentially taken place right under their noses without a single clue as to who had done it.

Simon and Ronnie discovered the climbing equipment was missing when the others went back to the main house.

"Do me a favour," Simon said to Ronnie. "Keep quiet about this missing gear like you did the cellar."

"Maybe he made it and is on his way back with help."

"Sure," Simon patted Ronnie on the arm.

Neither of them believed it though, their faces wouldn't lie for them.

III

As they ate, the politeness seemed forced. Satisfying hunger is a significant part of any survival strategy and the food acted like a civilised barrier. Suspicion erected its invisible barrier between each guest.

Terry was the last to make it to the breakfast room, having decided he needed to smoke on the narrow terrace circumnavigating the rear of the property.

Terry returned out of breath, his face sporting an unhealthy waxy sheen as pale as the window glass affording them a spectacular view of the Alps.

"What's the matter?" Jeff asked, getting up to greet him.

"Take your time," Patrick urged through a mouthful of cereal, instinctively getting out of his seat, such was the distress recorded on Terry's face.

Terry addressed all of them but looked to Jeff the whole time. He didn't know whether to refer to it as the statue or Anna or the corpse, or all three. He settled on the detachment of the statue.

"What about it?" Jeff said.

"She's whole again," Terry said. "Come see for yourselves. Someone's put her back together again."

IV

Anna greeted them, lit gloriously in the centre of the room by the natural light of the sun. Her face a vision of golden hues, making her appear almost alive. She was complete again, at least to somebody.

Anna was dead though, and her reappearance, her sudden resurrection once more, all the more unnerving for it spoke of genuine worship. Something past all normal reasoning.

Its dedicated restoration, a feat of skill and passion hidden by the night and aided by the fact that no-one but the killer wanted to go in there after the hideous events of the previous evening.

"This is one sick fuck," Jeff whispered to Terry, looking at Simon as he spoke. Terry nodded.

This illusion of Anna's resurrected life spoke of a serious intent on the part of the obsessed ex to see this through. Whoever reversed the damage Tony had done to her still wanted Anna all to himself. As crazy as that seemed.

"Somebody must have seen or heard something?" Grace said, looking around desperately.

But they hadn't, this was the shocking mockery to deal with. The audacity that somebody could have done all of this right under their noses. Carried it out without fear of being caught in the act.

It spoke of a shocking perceptiveness on the part of the ex that they would all retreat to their rooms during the night.

"Perhaps this is how he's to be caught," Ronnie suggested. "Through his obsession."

"Look at the craftsmanship." Dennis pointed out. "You can see he took his time to restore her."

It was true, the statue barely showed a scar at the neck.

The prize of Anna, still beautiful, kept on smiling back at them.

V

Understandably, the sight of Anna resurrected in this way deeply disturbed them, and solving the mystery of Jack's disappearance became even more important to Ronnie.

Ronnie asked Patrick about the psychological angle of the statue, but Patrick merely shook his head at the inquiry. He was either not at liberty to say or was still trying to fathom it out.

Or keeping that information to himself.

Ronnie thought that Patrick suddenly seemed cold and distant towards him as he exited the room with Simon.

Simon seized the initiative and took Patrick to one side in the library. Grace following them in.

"It's got to be him," Simon pleaded.

Patrick shook his head. Simon's theory was based on instinct rather than facts. Grace seemed to have been taken in by it, however, and this swayed Patrick, as Grace was nobody's fool.

"I don't know," Patrick said. "Give me time to think."

"We don't have time," Grace replied.

She held up her iPhone, the phone she couldn't get reception from. She explained that she had a signal in the cable car and confided in Simon by showing him the threatening e-mails.

"Simon showed me his e-mails too. Before we came up here, I mean. In our minds, that eliminates us. We don't suspect you."

"And some of the phrases he uses," Simon said, "they're the same as in the ex's e-mails."

106

"The same," Grace stressed.

Simon held up his hand, pulling a digit back. "Jack's a possibility but we'll leave him alone for now. Jeff's the only one who didn't register shock at Terry's revelation that the statue's head had been replaced."

"People exhibit shock in different ways," Patrick interrupted. "People are horrified and scared by different things. Maybe Jeff wasn't as shocked as the rest of us by the act. Or his shock registered later."

Neither Simon nor Grace were impressed with Patrick's theorising. They needed an ally, a conspirator, not someone to play devil's advocate. Someone who could tip Jeff off for what they had planned.

"Just hear us out," Grace said, grabbing Patrick's arm.

"I'm listening."

"All I'm saying is, let's keep a close watch on Jeff's movements tonight," Grace whispered. Simon nodded his agreement. Grace sighed. "It's our only option. You must see that?"

Simon took over as though they'd rehearsed this. "At least this way we have a chance to finish it once and for all."

Finally relenting, Patrick acknowledged their convincing argument for them working together as a threesome. Jeff's movements would be under surveillance from the three of them tonight, it was agreed.

"Just don't do anything rash," Patrick warned. "None of us are thinking straight."

"That's why we have to act now," Grace said. "It's only going to get worse when more bodies start turning up."

Patrick remained unconvinced Jeff was the homicidal type. Disturbed maybe, but not a murderer. But when pressed for an alternative, Patrick was unwilling to name a more likely suspect.

Patrick found a perverse excitement shared by Simon and Grace, though they would not admit it, of the academic puzzle it presented. The puzzle of human nature, or rather dysfunctional human nature.

The constant shifting of suspects in Simon's mind had settled on Jeff. Simon was convinced. He wanted his life back and perhaps after tonight, he'd have it.

Unmasking the ex, all three of them agreed, could only be achieved through being proactive with their suspicions.

Grace, equipped with the keen analytical mind of a medical doctor, and boasting years of responsible practice made Patrick think that Simon wouldn't be able to convince her to do something stupid. And Simon, he conceded, seemed to know a thing or two about the inner workings of the mind of this maniacal ex.

Perhaps he knows more than he's letting on, Patrick considered.

Their argument for suspecting Jeff was growing on him. Their logical argument was coercive to his professional mind.

"Listen to some of the phrases he uses," Grace reminded him. "Think back to the disturbing e-mails sent to you. It's him. It has to be."

CHAPTER TEN

I

When Patrick met Jeff and Terry in the living room, Jeff's eyes narrowed and he cocked his head in an intimidating manner as if he were sizing Patrick up. As if he'd already got wise to the plot against him. He was looking at Jeff in a whole new light, none of it particularly flattering. Perhaps Grace and Simon were right. There was something not quite right about Jeff, or Terry for that matter. Something behind their eyes.

Jeff whispered in Terry's ear and Terry nodded. His look as unashamedly cold as Jeff's was towards Patrick.

Patrick retreated onto the glass terrace, looking over his shoulder. They were still following him. Patrick found himself unable to resist peering over the unfathomable edge. He hadn't felt vertigo like this since he was a boy. When he glanced back, they were still watching him with menacing eyes.

He had to find the others.

II

It was gone 1 pm when a civilised group meeting finished, all agreeing that their unknown nemesis would not take any chances during the day.

Nightfall hours away still, they all developed their own way of easing the tension. Patrick and Grace read paperbacks, their faces serene, as did Dennis but with a grumpy look pinching his brow throughout. Terry and Jeff continued to bond over the pool table, while Simon patiently assisted Ronnie in his fruitless search for Jack that took them over every square foot of the house and grounds again.

III

Patrick was transfixed. She could still draw him in with her natural beauty alone, even now she was dead. He reached out a shaking hand to touch her, withdrawing it before he felt the cold embrace of the statue. Dust motes framed her like dancing fairies in this stolen fantasyland he would allow himself only for a moment.

"Anna," he said softly.

She was dead, this illusion of life a cruel trick. He hadn't realised a tear had slipped down his cheek until a voice startled him, speaking Anna's name.

"We're all puppets to desire when we get down to it, aren't we?" Dennis said, entering the room. His sunglasses, the same Ray-Bans brand as Jack's, hid his eyes. "Pathetic really."

Patrick, now in control of his emotions, nodded slowly.

"This is why we all came here. God, you forget just how beautiful she is... was, I mean."

Patrick was not disagreeing with him in his silence.

"I've tried many times to capture this beauty on the page and failed," Dennis admitted, going one step further and delicately stroking her cheek, before thinking better of it. "Perhaps I shouldn't touch her, evidence and all that – I didn't think."

Remaining statuesque himself, Patrick didn't comment on it. Patrick was not listening. Anna's beauty had been captured in this statue like a rare insect drowned in amber so that her form could be studied and defined by someone who would never understand it. He wouldn't let their love be reduced to that. He abruptly turned and left without a word, leaving Dennis to his private worship.

Dennis spoke on for a time, not realising, in his trance, that the psychiatrist had left until he turned his head in Patrick's direction to ask a question. The question that went unanswered was: would Patrick admit to being relieved that she wasn't still alive to be pursued?

Dennis put the same question to the statue of Anna instead of Patrick.

It was getting dark outside, and they were only hours away from yet another shocking revelation of Anna's mysterious life. Even in death, she was still dominating their thoughts and actions. This made Dennis – rooted to the spot by her – consider the question of who exactly was trapped by whom here.

IV

As a doctor, she knew she shouldn't be thinking like this. It was unbecoming of her profession. What would they think of her? Her oath was to preserve life, not take it. But she was so sure it was him. It all added up, what Anna had said, what Patrick had said, what she had mistrusted in his eyes. Jeff was the one that had to die. One quick dosage would do it. Her excuse was that the death would be, if not painless, at least over quickly. A further excuse that she would be preserving life in doing so. Saving six more lives with the act. There would be another death tonight unless she acted quickly. But Grace knew deep down that this was no excuse. No justification for taking a life.

Grace put the vial away in her drawer, dismissing the idea with a shake of her head. No excuse at all. She'd just wait it out.

V

Approaching minus twenty outside, it was too cold to smoke. Two voices conspired in the darkness as the wind tore strips from exposed skin like a silent, ruthless assassin who would never stop.

A few lights were still on this side of the house, but they knew they couldn't be seen. More importantly, they knew they couldn't be heard over the wind.

"What if we're wrong about him?" Terry said. "It's risky."

"My risk to take," Jeff replied, steely determination etched on his face.

"I'm not sure this is going to work."

"It will."

VI

Snow fell heavily, isolating them further.

Ronnie was all alone in Jack's room taking another sip of his J&B whisky. Jack had left the whisky along with half his clothes.

"It makes no sense," Ronnie said quietly to himself. "No sense at all."

Unless you're dead.

They'd all given up on the search he was still performing. Was that because they all knew something he didn't? No, that was paranoia setting in again. There was one of them who knew of Jack's exact whereabouts though, and this was not paranoia.

Only Simon had assisted him in his search and he got the impression that he had only done so for his own sake. Simon still suspected Jack of being in hiding, that had been obvious, despite Simon's efforts to hide it. Simon had confided in Ronnie yesterday that he suspected Jeff was involved somehow. Did that mean that he suspected Jack of being his accomplice?

Had Simon been sent on a mission by Patrick and Grace though? That was what troubled Ronnie over Simon's willingness to tag along.

With Jack's disappearance, Ronnie reflected that he had become the most isolated figure in the house. Grace, Patrick and Simon had allied. Terry and Jeff were inseparable over their endless pool sessions and suspicious looks. Dennis loitered freely between both camps, accepted and unsuspected by both parties. This meant Ronnie was in present danger as the outsider.

Ronnie had searched the kitchen for a knife before coming here but found that they had all gone.

Even with the lights on, it was as dark in here. *So goddamned dark and depressing*, Ronnie cursed to himself.

But that is how the house had been designed. As dark and mysterious as its owner. Its calculation gave him an inner chill, designed at every corner to mask an approach. Or an attack. It was a thought so disturbing that once formed could not be dispelled easily.

Ronnie counteracted this only with another gulp of whisky which warmed his innards like a slow-burning furnace, its' comforting heat seeping deep down his throat and into his belly. That sip would be his last though, any more alcohol would slow down his survival wits, wits which fed on his anxiety.

But the whisky was helping him to think. He could take a little more, he reassured himself.

He'd been over every square foot of the house looking for hidden recesses. Any disguised passageway or storage space where Jack could be dead or dying.

He'd left half of this whisky bottle along with half his belongings. It made no sense to Ronnie.

"Why would you do that, Jack?" Ronnie asked himself again, taking another sip of the whisky that was made for this climate. "Why?"

Ronnie still didn't know whom to suspect or why and that was the root of his anxiety.

His anxiety went up another notch as he sensed he was being watched.

Ronnie spun around.

In the open doorway, a silhouetted figure studied him. A man's distinctive broad-shouldered form. Ronnie squinted, but only this man's outline was clear against the meagre light provided by the bulb's dim wattage.

The dark figure was holding something in his hand. Something described in a long stretching shadow that almost reached Ronnie. The shadow long and thin and sharp.

Ronnie now knew why there were no knives to be found in the kitchen.

Chapter Eleven

I

Jeff could not find Terry anywhere. He called out again. This he found odd, as they'd agreed to stick together at all times. This was taking an unnecessary risk.

"Terry," Jeff hissed.

No answer.

Jeff felt that someone was watching him. At the end of the corridor he could make out a shape that could have been a man, but it was too dimly lit to be certain.

"Terry, is that you?"

Jeff realised it wasn't Terry as the figure shot into life, running towards him.

Jeff retreated down a long winding corridor, aware the whole time that his pursuer was closing the gap.

Jeff spun around, poised to fight.

No one there.

Out of the shadows, a figure pounced on him, knocking Jeff to the floor.

II

"You're the last person I suspected," Ronnie eyed Patrick with caution.

"Oh this," Patrick looked down at the knife he held tightly. "Everybody needs protection."

"That's all it is?"

"That's all."

"Why don't you put it down then," Ronnie said, his voice tight.

Patrick looked down at the blade by his side, "not just yet."

III

The two men grappled, clawing at each other. Jeff strong enough, barely, to keep his man at bay as they rolled over. In the darkness, Jeff couldn't get a look at his attacker's face, but he didn't need to. He knew his attacker was the man he suspected of being the killer all along.

As Jeff's assailant started to overpower him, he screamed Terry's name.

Terry was Jeff's only hope now.

IV

They stood for what seemed like an age in Jack's room as a ruckus broke out elsewhere in the house. It sounded like a fight on the floor below them.

Patrick looked back for a moment, thought about leaving, and instead kept Ronnie penned in. Patrick knew he couldn't back out now, he was committed to going through with it.

Both Ronnie and Patrick heard footsteps downstairs, and a slamming of the front door. Had the others gone outside? Were they all alone?

"One thing you didn't say," Ronnie said. "One omission that made me consider you as the killer."

"That's interesting. What?"

Ronnie coughed. "You told us that dangerous schizophrenics often form an elaborate delusional world where they're the victims, right?"

"What about it?"

"What you neglected to say was the other major common symptom of paranoid schizophrenia."

"Enlighten me."

"Paranoid schizophrenics hold another common belief. An unwavering belief that they're in a position of authority and they," Ronnie raised a finger for emphasis just as he did when lecturing a class on an important point to remember. "And only they, know the real truth. And they trust nobody."

Ronnie fumbled for the glass ashtray on the bedside table, finding it without taking his eyes off Patrick. The ashtray didn't weigh enough to crack a skull. Both men's faces seemed to instantly appreciate that fact.

"I agree with that general diagnosis, yes," Patrick answered calmly, his lips breaking into a smile. "But you can appreciate why I didn't share that information with everyone."

"I don't follow."

"Well," Patrick smiled again. "None of us trusts anybody here, do we?"

Ronnie considered this as he gripped the ashtray tighter.

V

Terry sprung from hiding, just as they had arranged. Dennis not far behind.

Dennis held Jeff's attacker's leg as Terry turned him over onto his back, pinning his arm at an unnatural angle in the process. The attacker exhaled a sharp breath with the sudden pain in his shoulder.

They dragged Jeff's aggressor out into the light.

"About fuckin' time," Jeff hissed. "Jesus."

It was no surprise to any of them to see Simon's resentful features leering back at them.

They finally had this maniac right where the wanted him.

There would be no more games. The ex, after all of his careful planning, had finally tripped up with the ambitiousness of his plan here.

"Get off me," Simon grunted, as he wriggled in an attempt to break free. His flushed face contorted to ugliness in its straining, a delta of veins forming on his forehead. "What the hell do you think you're doing? Get off of me now!"

They were, unsurprisingly, unwilling to do this.

Chapter Twelve

I

"It makes no sense, whatsoever," Grace said. "What's his motive?"

"It makes perfect sense to me," Jeff said.

"It would," Grace scoffed.

Grace was growing infuriated with the situation, as they held Simon down. Not letting him breathe. She wanted Patrick to back her up but Patrick was nowhere to be found. Nor Ronnie. Two people, she was relying on to make this rabble see sense.

"Can't you see he was just defending himself?" Grace said.

"Defending himself, right," Terry shouted, drawing himself up to his full height. "I saw him advance on Jeff. I saw the knife."

"How could you? You said it was dark." Grace said, throwing her hands up with the helplessness of her situation. "And we've all got knives,"

She called out Patrick's name again, still no answer.

"I saw it too," Dennis said.

Dennis backed Terry up, of course. She knew he would. *What a two-faced little weasel he'd turned out to be*, Grace seethed. *Simon had been right about him.*

"What're we going to do now?" Dennis said.

Jeff produced a brass key from the back pocket of his Wranglers.

"What's that?" Grace asked.

"The key to the equipment shed," Jeff said.

"You can't lock him in there," Grace pleaded, alone in her outrage. Never so desperate. Never so helplessly surrounded by toxic idiots.

"I thought he was going to kill me," Simon pleaded, his voice groggy from the working over they'd given him. A working over (from Terry and then Jeff) that had formed a blood goatee around his chin. His nose still streaming in deep red rivulets. "He'd been following *me*."

"Shut it you," Jeff said.

Simon collapsed to one knee as they pushed him down, dragging him out of the front door and into the gnawing wind and snow.

"Hey, I was trying to treat his wounds," Grace yelled as Dennis cordoned her off at the doorway with his arm.

"Sorry, Doc."

"Don't be sorry, just get out of my way."

"Can't, I'm afraid," Dennis didn't budge.

The journey to the equipment shed was mercifully short in distance, but even in this brief time, the wind chill factor was biting into exposed skin. The equipment shed, being an outhouse building, had no heating and seemed as cool as a fridge.

"You can't do this. It's not right," Grace shouted, pushing past Dennis and tugging at Jeff's arm.

Jeff shrugged her off, "just watch me."

II

Five minutes later Simon was locked up in the equipment shed. Blankets, bottles of water and tinned fruit his only supplies. Thick oak double doors penned him in with three sides of stone masonry that was between two and three feet thick. Short of tunnelling under the walls, escape would be extremely difficult.

Jeff was certain he'd got his man. Simon had behaved just as predicted, and Jeff's conviction in this regard persuaded the others. There was no turning back now. They were already assigning shifts to keep watch over the equipment shed from the glass terrace. Hourly checks were to be made at the door of the equipment shed to confirm he hadn't escaped.

Grace pleaded Simon's innocence. That she hadn't witnessed the scene herself took her authority away from her, her doctor's authority over these men.

They were utterly convinced. She'd only been surprised at what a fool Simon had been to pull this stunt. She'd expected more from him. Perhaps he wasn't the man she thought he was.

Other than herself, it was only Patrick who suspected Jeff to be something other than what he was letting on, and she knew she was right about Jeff and the danger he presented. Never more so than now and the twist tonight's events had thrown up. Everyone suddenly taking Jeff's lead.

Patrick had agreed with her suspicions of Jeff's growing instability, and from the clinical perspective of a psychiatrist too.

Only Patrick was nowhere to be found.

III

He's not going to let me out of this room.

"You suspect Jeff, don't you?" Ronnie said to Patrick. "But you're not positive, hence..." Ronnie made nervous eyes at the steak knife.

When Patrick didn't answer, Ronnie said hoarsely, "You're wrong."

"Who do you think it is then?"

"Not you, not really. At least I didn't until you pulled this stunt."

"It's necessary for me to establish a detail or two in my mind until I can eliminate you."

Ronnie didn't like the word 'eliminate' under the circumstances. Nor did he care for the cold, detached emphasis Patrick had put on it. He'd not seen this side of Patrick before. His face had become creepily vacant.

"Ask away," Ronnie replied with a lump in his throat. The psycho was going to ask him about Anna, he was sure.

"No questions," Patrick's bushy brows converged. "It's rather a case of what you have to do to prove to me that you're not him."

The control in his voice, suddenly sadistic to Patrick himself, made it clear that he would not let Ronnie out of this room until he'd made Ronnie prove he was not the ex.

After what seemed like a full minute had passed, Ronnie heard stamping feet and excited voices carrying. His voice faint and laboured with the rising tension, Ronnie said, "What's all that commotion about?" He made eyes at the hallway.

The question went unanswered, Patrick still blocking the doorway. "As you said, I may be wrong about Jeff."

Patrick took a breath as he laid out his plan to Ronnie. Ronnie sensed Patrick was on edge too. *Nervous of getting caught? Or excited by the prospect of killing him?*

"We both distinctively heard the others go outside for whatever reason," Patrick finally spoke again. "We're all alone, yes?"

Ronnie nodded.

"I can eliminate you and you can eliminate me if you do this one thing."

"Come towards you," Ronnie said. "That's what you mean, isn't it? A kind of leap of faith." Ronnie surprised himself by letting out a nervous laugh he barely recognised as his own. "You don't ask for much, do you?"

Ronnie looked Patrick in the eye, deciding to take the first step.

Ronnie was poised to take a second step, making a conscious effort to achieve the walk towards the doorway and Patrick, only Ronnie's feet all of a sudden remained stubbornly planted in the thick carpet.

He believed that Patrick was not the homicidal killer hiding amongst them.

Only he didn't believe enough to take that second step.

IV

"Look, if the killing doesn't stop," Jeff said. "I'll let him out. I promise"

He spoke with a finality he hoped to close the matter on.

"Under the circumstances, that's fair enough," Terry backed Jeff up, rubbing his hands now that they were back in the warmth of the house.

"Is it fair that he dies of hypothermia in the meantime?!" Grace said.

"He won't," Jeff replied.

"I'm the doctor!" Grace roared at Jeff, but looking at all of them with disgust.

"I want that key now," Grace said. "Hand it over, I insist."

"Out of the question," Jeff said.

"Give me the key."

"I threw it over the mountainside, I'm afraid." Jeff smiled and left, his pal Terry following him.

"It's what's known as locking them up and throwing away the key." Grace could hear an echoing Jeff tell Terry with undisguised smug satisfaction in his voice. They were heading for the kitchen for supplies before another of their marathon pool sessions where they plotted their next move.

"Even that's too good for that sick bastard," Terry said.

"Grace doesn't think so," she could hear Dennis say as he joined them.

"We'll soon see," Jeff said. "They'll be no more killing tonight. Or tomorrow, or the next day." Jeff put a hand on Terry's shoulder. "It's over, mate."

Dennis came back into the room to witness a defeated looking Grace slump into a chair. Grace felt that she had been punched in the stomach with Jeff's revelation that the key was lost, voicing to Dennis that he shouldn't trust Jeff as he was mentally unstable. Patrick had noted Jeff's instability too, Dennis must speak with Patrick about it if he didn't believe her.

Grace carried on pleading with Dennis, drawing parallels to the witch trials when the accused were found to be innocent only after they had drowned.

It was madness, utter madness.

Dennis ignored all the melodrama, his mind made up. Fear had hardened him. "Those walls are thick enough for him to survive under the blankets we gave him, Doc. He won't die."

"He might."

Dennis shook his head as he left the room, "it's the only way, Doc."

Grace, alone and in tears now, swore obscenities at Dennis as Patrick came down the stairs, passing him.

"What's happened to Simon?" Patrick asked with a blank expression on his face.

Grace, her face buried in her hands, couldn't answer him for a long time.

V

Five of them breakfasted together, united by the fact that no one had died last night. Only Grace had ventured out to talk to Simon this morning (or rather to talk to him through the oak doors, at least) and was still unconvinced that he was the ex. This was just a ploy by the killer to kill again, inducing hypothermia in his calculating idleness. He didn't have to do a thing this time, the bloody fools. That's what she'd told them. Then after a day or two, with Simon dead, and with their guards lowered, someone else would be murdered, she had no doubts.

By late evening, if the 'internal weather' of the house had settled this was not the case outside, as a blizzard was clearly on the way. But for the present, they could believe that they were at least in the picturesque Tyrolese Alps and not in a prison where only cruelty and death was to be found at every stranded turn.

There was still tension between Grace and Jeff, but nothing like there had been. The wound Simon had inflicted had bled through two layers of bandaging and had betrayed Jeff's attestation of it being a mere "flesh wound." The constant ache had done nothing for Jeff's pool playing or his mood.

Jeff winced as he clasped his wounded shoulder again. He was multi-tasking by sipping beer and having to manoeuvre his cutlery with just the one hand at dinner. That there were only blunt knives left in the kitchen made the job that much harder. He would not accept assistance either.

"You should let me take a look at that," Grace said.

Jeff shook his head.

"Look, it might become infected. If it isn't already."

"I'll survive, Doc."

Someone at the table, of course, doubted that fact.

"One more of us acquitted – too late!"

Agatha Christie, *And Then There Were None*

Part 3

Ronnie

CHAPTER THIRTEEN

I

The exact time of death could not be determined. At least, not in any practical sense that would provide any of them with an alibi. Grace was a GP, not a pathologist. She had made that quite clear.

The shiny chrome dumbbell rested a foot behind Ronnie's head, propped on the side of the Jacuzzi. The dumbbell spattered with dried blood and hair at one end. That had been the weapon used to knock Ronnie out cold. The neat incision at his throat was from a knife still to be found.

Terry was examining him under Jeff's directions.

"Terry was a paramedic," Jeff said, looking smugly at Grace with this revelation.

"He's already dead in case you haven't noticed," Dennis replied sarcastically, which did him no favours with anyone.

Terry lifted Ronnie's eyelids. "He was drugged, I think."

"You all know that he consulted me for his insomnia, so you might as well come out and say it," Grace said, her eyes narrowing.

Patrick, uncharacteristically quiet until now spoke with conviction. Patrick subconsciously spread his palms as if in apology for asking the question he knew he had to ask. "What exactly did you treat him with?"

"The usual. Firstly, I told him to cut his caffeine intake, particularly before bedtime – the coffee and the diet Coke he drank, the obvious."

"Yes, but *what* did you prescribe him with?" Terry said.

Jeff folded his arms, a slow smile forming on his lips.

"I was just getting to that. When he still complained, I detected from what he told me that his histamine levels were high, giving him prolonged bouts of restlessness."

"What did you give him?" Jeff asked impatiently.

"I gave him some of the Nytol I had with me. It's an over-the-counter remedy, I'm sure you've seen 'the Good Night-all' adverts… its active ingredient is Diphenhydramine."

"Could he have overdosed on it?" Patrick inquired, unable to resist stroking his chin.

"Not a chance."

"Mixed with something else," Terry added.

"And that something else would be…" Grace responded in her defence.

"He wouldn't have accidentally overdosed?" Patrick inquired with a gentility Grace did not pick up on.

"What he's asking for is because we've all concluded that you happened on the body," Jeff said, taking over. Speaking in the manner of a prosecuting lawyer honing his sentences, waiting for Grace to trip herself up. "That you, seeing that Ronnie had drowned, tried to make an accidental death look like murder for Simon's sake."

"Look," Grace said, her voice rising with every word. "He taught chemistry, for Christ's sake. He knew what he was taking. And drowning in a jacuzzi, does that sound likely to you?"

"Even so."

"As I say, he had been a chemist. Someone murdered him." She paused for effect. "One of you."

II

The blizzard outside had pressed their sanity further, heightening the cabin fever as its cold fury blew a ghostlike taunt around the house walls.

No matter how unreal this all seemed, no one gave credence to the claim that Grace had happened upon an already dead Ronnie and tried to make it look like murder, botching it with the blow to the head and the slit throat.

The killer wanted to give this impression, to lay a seed of doubt. He was that clever.

They were slowly starting to concede that this killer – the ex – was still in the house. Was in all probability one of the four men discussing it now. That was the disturbing fact they had to face all over again.

Jeff spoke, thinking aloud, "The killer crept down here, worked him over with a dumbbell." They all looked down at the incriminating weapon. "Slit his throat with a knife while he was semi-conscious, and in all likelihood drugged him first as a precaution." He shook his head. "It doesn't work for me. Unless…"

"We've been over and over this," Dennis said impatiently. "Just do us all a favour and say what you mean. You usually don't have a problem with that, Jeff."

Jeff unconsciously widened his shoulders. "Whoever did this. They weren't taking any chances. That's what I'm saying."

"I'll save you the bother. I think we all know where this is headed," Grace said in a tired tone. "What Sherlock is implying is that a woman did it. Me."

There was a long, uncomfortable silence. They all looked down at the pink water that looked as though Ronnie had been boiled alive. Dennis thought to mention that the knife was probably at the bottom of the Jacuzzi, making the act over in a matter of seconds, and the incriminating evidence untraceable, but it served no purpose to do so.

Perhaps the killer was disturbed in the act was what everyone was thinking. This was not the outside world where they had to worry about fingerprints and DNA matches.

That seemed crucial.

Whatever angle you came at this death, it did not make any sense. Maybe that was the whole point, the brilliance of it. They all suspected each other still and with no credible motive behind their suspicions.

"The ex, in case you have forgotten, was a man, geniuses." Grace huffed, making for the stairs. Jeff thought about putting out a hand to stop her as she passed him but decided to let her leave.

"Where're you off to?" Terry asked.

"Where do you think?" Grace said. "Ronnie's death clears him."

"Don't be a fool," Terry said. "No one's going out in this."

III

Grace, to give her credit, attempted to go out in the blizzard but retreated shortly afterwards, finally seeing sense. Her doctor's common sense.

The slanting wind raked across the fifty yards of open space to the equipment shed. The equipment shed teetered on the edge of a sheer drop, this factor more than anything else deterring her. She and anyone with her could easily be swept off the mountainside in these brutal conditions.

There was no way to get to Simon.

Another planned murder had been successfully executed.

IV

Dennis looked at his bedside clock. It was after 2 am.

His cure for insomnia had always been a bloody good story. After half an hour or so of reading he was relaxed enough to drop into a deep sleep.

He had been reading a lot of science-fiction lately because the latest crime novel he'd outlined before coming out here was a murder investigation taking place on the set of a Hollywood sci-fi movie. Its lead detective instructed to be more character-driven and more unassuming than Chief Inspector Dawson, on his agent's sound advice. He read Philip K. Dick's, *A Maze of Death*, a book he'd conveniently found in his bedside table drawer. In the novel, fourteen people arrive on the strange plains of Delmak-0 where one by one they are murdered by a mysterious presence.

Just like in this house.

To Die For

He finally put the book down, three more characters dead. He'd had enough of fiction for one night as he yawned. He'd thought about his next book being non-fiction.

Dennis had it all laid out in his mind's eye, a non-fiction piece on the events of the recent stage tragedy. Including linking it to this little episode through Simon's involvement. If he survived.

That sort of non-fiction was always hot. The type of book that sold regardless of its quality. At this stage in his career that was precisely what he needed.

Look at all those Jack the Ripper speculators he'd read over the years with a raised eyebrow throughout but revisited.

With the possible exception of the conspiracy surrounding Brandon Lee, this recent West End scandal represented the most notorious death on a stage or movie set of his generation. The stage actor's death – unlike Lee's – was unquestionably foul play and not in any interpretable way accidental. It would intrigue for years to come, certainly more than another Dawson outing would.

This non-fiction piece would be something to be read with a raised eyebrow but read nevertheless. A speculator and if not an overnight bestseller, certainly a seller.

If delving into the lives of notorious real-life suspects sold books, celebrity suspects certainly would. The scandal of the century by the time he'd finished with it. Meeting one of the suspects here had given him an angle as well. A unique perspective. He'd write it.

All he had to do was survive.

And ensure Simon did too.

V

There were no accidents in life, Dennis was starting to agree. Dawson would certainly agree. Him meeting Simon was no accident either.

Dennis looked out at the snow-covered equipment shed from his bedroom window, the backdrop of the Alps like a movie set.

Knowing his luck, he'd get out there only to find Simon dead. Frozen to death. They hadn't been able to get to him yet because of this unending blizzard and its rather inconvenient timing keeping them from rescuing an innocent man. He wouldn't bet against the killer getting to him in that locked outhouse building first. He'd proved superhuman so far. An efficient killing machine.

Dennis would have written about the ex, but he was still too unbelievable to be able to write as a credible character. Still too unbelievable to suspect or detect even now. Which meant he was too elusive to even begin to imagine.

If he'd written any of this, the critics would have slated him, and yet here he was living it.

"Everyone's a critic nowadays," Dennis said to himself. "Especially the writer."

That was the advantage of non-fiction, it didn't have to be plausible. It didn't have to be wrapped up all neat and tidy with a bow. This, from a writing perspective, was yet another paradox for him to outline as a major theme.

"Paradoxes don't sell," he said to himself, smiling. "Accusations do. Scandalous accusations."

Dawson wouldn't have approved of the absence of tidy logic in this case. Not one bit.

Dawson wouldn't have approved of him suspecting Jeff without a shred of evidence against him either.

Dawson wouldn't have approved of the knife in his hand now.

Dawson never approved of anything.

That was why he had to kill Dawson off.

And if he listened to Dawson, he'd be dead too.

Dennis propped his pillows under the tight bedsheets to make a lumpy outline of his form at rest. He settled into the reclining chair in the corner. Settling down into the comfort of darkness.

Dennis found he couldn't take his eyes off the door. After a time, his eyelids inevitably closed in sleep.

VI

Dennis woke in the chair in the corner of his bedroom.

Dennis had been a light sleeper since he'd arrived here and he'd awoken just half an hour later he saw by the illuminating light on his watch. Groggy and disorientated, he heard footsteps outside his door. A door, Dennis recognised, was now ajar.

Dennis reached down, but the knife was no longer in his lap.

Chapter Fourteen

I

"Missing something, Dennis?" An unrecognisable voice asked in the darkness.

The whispering, ghost-like voice close by.

In the room somewhere.

Behind him.

Dennis felt cool steel press against his bobbing Adam's apple. The Blade close enough to his skin that he couldn't hope to move or even talk without it cutting into him.

"This what you came for, darling?" It was Anna's voice. Sweet and light and completely at odds with the situation he was in.

Dennis felt the razor-sharp knife's edge slice his throat as a shower of hot blood covered his toes, his scream silent as he cupped his gushing neck. The only noise was the tinkling sound when he missed the toilet bowl and peed on the seat. This absurd sound (and thought) to be his last memory as he became weak.

Dennis shook spasmodically as he woke with a start in the chair, the knife overbalancing in his lap as his reality had moments earlier.

"Open up," an insistent voice whispered. A deep male voice this time.

Patrick's?

Or Jeff's impersonation of it? Jeff could mimic all their accents. That had been his party piece on the first evening. Dennis wouldn't fall for it. He wasn't opening his door, relieved to find it was locked in reality.

"Go back to bed!" Dennis shouted through the door. "I'm not coming out."

Only when Grace's and Terry's voices accompanied what was now clearly Patrick's posh accent, did Dennis turn on the lights and open his door.

"The storm's died down a bit," Patrick said, with a conviction that didn't ring true on his or the others' weary faces. "We're going to get Simon."

Dennis reached for his Billabong jacket, hat and gloves hanging on the radiator.

"Count me in."

II

Grace, Patrick and Terry formed a new alliance as they braved what was still a blizzard by English weather standards but mild in comparison to yesterday's record-breaking conditions.

A low sun peeking over the Alps meant that they could at least make out the general direction of where they were heading, but the wind remained a brutal blur of whirling snow cutting down their visibility as it stung their eyes.

Dennis remained behind to guard against Jeff locking them out of the house. Dennis had enjoyed the most success in reasoning with Jeff so far.

This was because Jeff didn't see Dennis as a threat, Patrick theorised. *They could use that.*

Dennis didn't disagree with him, happy to remain indoors.

"Stay by the door, and if you feel you're in danger," Grace said, "yell for us."

"If it comes to it, for God's sake just leave the house," Patrick said, offering his support. "We'll work a way to get back inside later."

"There's four of us remember," Terry agreed, patting Dennis on the shoulder. "And only one of him."

So, Terry believes that Jeff is the killer too now, Dennis acknowledged. *Probably why he isn't staying behind with me.*

Dennis, sipping a gin and tonic on the porch, watched their steady progress through the thick blanket of snow as he ran this detail over in his mind. It was proving to be slow going to the equipment shed and (a hopefully still breathing) Simon.

Dennis looked over his shoulder now and again, acutely aware that Jeff was somewhere in the house.

The steak knife in his pocket felt like little insurance.

Jeff had his hunting knife.

III

Though his suspicions of Jeff had never been stronger, Dennis didn't rule out that one of the three of them wading through the snow at the edge of a sheer drop wouldn't shove the other two off the mountainside and announce themselves in the most frightening fashion imaginable. With this psycho, you couldn't rule anything out.

To Die For

If this were the case, all he would have to do is shut this iron-studded oak monster of a front door, bolt and lock it. Let the elements take care of the rest. There would be a way in through the windows of course, and the glass conservatory, but he would be waiting there for them. He considered for a moment bolting and locking it anyway, his self-preservation at its ugliest.

It was then that Dennis heard movement, someone creeping behind him.

Dennis turned around, poised for an attack.

"Nothing," he said to himself in a whisper.

His second or third G&T of the morning (after a heavy night of drinking) taking effect on his imagination?

"You're losing it," he muttered to himself. "Definitely losing it."

Dennis had to keep mentally slapping himself to concentrate on the here and now. He heard a stair creak and reeled so fast that he lost his footing and spilt the dregs of his precious gin and tonic.

"Shit," he said, clasping an empty glass. "Well done, Dennis."

He looked resentfully up at the empty stairs. "And guess what? There's no one there, you idiot."

And yet he still felt he was being watched, but that was nothing new. He'd lived with that trapped, hunted feeling ever since Anna had introduced him to the story of her stalking ex. Told on a sleepless night that was to be the accompanied by many to come.

A problem shared was not a burden halved in this case, it was a burden doubled. Cheers Anna.

Dennis had lived this fear through his novels too, the feeling of being stalked a common theme in his work since.

He'd used its creative juices to spawn half a dozen Dawson mysteries. The stalking ex leaving him alone for spells as long as a couple of years at a time. A time in which to concentrate his preying personality on the other members of this crazed household he now realised.

The brave rescue party of three was almost at the door of the equipment shed. The equipment shed where Simon was being kept. Terry had somehow got the key off Jeff who had lied about throwing it over the mountainside.

Dennis believed Jeff kept the key only for the reassurance later that Simon had starved or been frozen to death in that equipment shed. Jeff was not a good guy.

Jeff's drunken slur bellowed out, making Dennis jump. "What the fuck do they think they're doing?"

Jeff slowly descended the stairs, his hand never parting from the rail. "Fucking answer me, Dennis."

"Simon," Dennis said, hearing his voice tremble beyond recognition. "They're rescuing Simon."

"I see," the hunting knife Jeff held scraped the bannister wood in a screech as he stumbled. For some odd reason, Jeff held one hand behind his back, which affected his balance.

"That motherfucker double-crossed me. He'll pay for that."

IV

The key didn't fit the lock to the equipment shed.

"What do we do now?" Patrick said, but before he could finish his sentence Terry came forward with his axe.

The axe crashed through the equipment shed door. The fifth or sixth blow shattered the centre panelling, and a few seconds later Terry heaved and lodged the door off its hinges. Finally, they had reached Simon.

Only the room was empty.

V

"The motherfucker took the key while I was out cold," a drunken Jeff roared the accusation at Dennis.

'The motherfucker' Dennis could only deduce meant his one-time buddy Terry. Jeff was moving extremely slowly, staggering as if he too were outside in the blizzard.

"I didn't," Dennis protested.

"You didn't what?"

"I didn't betray you."

"Betray me?" Jeff became even angrier. "You've all betrayed me. Be a man about it."

"He's here!" Dennis tried to shout out but found he had no voice to match the wind outside. He raised his arms, waving them frantically in a distress signal, but they weren't looking in his direction.

"I found this," Jeff said, pocketing his hunting knife and brandishing a blade several times its length. "Hanging in the study."

"Jesus Christ!" Dennis said when Jeff raised a gleaming samurai sword above his head.

"This is the only way to be sure," Jeff threatened with a whisper, stepping closer. "And that includes you, Dennis."

VI

The room wasn't empty, they found Simon crumpled in a heap in the corner of the equipment shed, hiding under blankets and anything he could find to insulate himself. There looked to be about as much life in his face as there was in the statue of Anna. They helped his limp body up, afraid that he'd stop breathing. Patrick threw his coat over him. After what seemed like an age, Grace found a faint pulse.

"If he dies it's murder," Grace said.

VII

Dennis wanted to go out into the blizzard but knew he couldn't in case Jeff locked them all out.

That, after all, was why he remained here. He reached for the knife concealed in his jacket pocket and even this movement felt clumsy. He would be no match for Jeff with a sword.

He would have to reason with him, he stood a better chance of doing that than fighting Jeff.

Jeff was drunk and didn't know what he was saying or doing though.

It's just an act, Dennis feared. *Jeff's going to spring alive at any moment.*

But he was in full view of the others who'd almost covered half their journey back to the house. Jeff wouldn't kill him in front of the others. That wasn't the style of the ex. Each murder had to go undetected.

"He's here!" Dennis screamed, amazed that they still couldn't hear him.

Jeff dragged a foot on the marble chessboard flooring, resembling Jack Torrence in *The Shining*. Spotting the others, he surprised Dennis by lowering his sword and retreating into the house.

Instructions were barked outside by Grace as Dennis stared at the body they were carrying. Simon's face whiter and possibly colder than the snow outside, indicated that his condition was every bit as critical as Grace had feared.

Dennis looked behind him and Jeff was gone as if he had never been there. The only one in mortal danger now was Simon. According to Grace's instructions they had to act now if they were to save him.

VIII

"Stay with me, Simon," Grace whispered.

Simon was barely conscious, his mumbled words making no sense as they stripped him of his damp clothes and towelled his naked body down before putting two layers of fresh, dry clothing on him. Simon's breathing remained shallow and erratic throughout.

"Stay with me now."

Dennis saw that his hands and feet looked the palest, a lifeless blue-purple as Grace rubbed them to get blood vessels to flow again. She didn't like the dilation of the pupils nor his lagging pulse rate.

"Anything I can do?" Dennis asked.

"Just keep out of my way. Leave me alone with him."

"Of course, Doc."

Over the next few hours, they gave him warmed bottled water, as Grace instructed them that tea, coffee or whisky would only dehydrate him further. He was spoon-fed soup by Grace at six, unable to sit up straight himself to take the sustenance.

Grace seemed keen to be alone with him, and the others were happy for her to have her wish. Simon's possible death to the elements was a reminder of their precarious mortality, and being cut off from a civilisation they might not ever return to.

They reflected on a life they'd given up so freely. So freely for a love, they'd travelled halfway across Europe to be reunited with only to find her to be reduced to a hideous carnival exhibit on their first evening here. A joke for a sick but keener mind.

How could a mind like that outthink them at every turn and still be termed sick? Patrick had wondered.

Terry explained the update on Simon's condition to Dennis and Patrick at dinner, drawing on all his paramedic knowledge, though Dennis suspected he'd been spoon-fed most of it by Grace as she had spoon-fed the soup to a shivering Simon. Grace had also told them to keep an eye out for Jeff. She could be clever like that when she wanted to be, devious even.

She wanted Jeff dead now.

IX

To Die For

Hypothermia occurs when the body dips below thirty-five degrees. Dennis knew this much from a novel he'd set in Antarctica.

If Simon's core temperature dropped below thirty-four degrees and he curled up in a foetal position, as his muscles became rigid, and his pulse rate dropped, it could become fatal. Grace later explained all this to them.

Patrick asked if this was the condition referred to as 'the metabolic icebox,' to which Terry was unsure. Grace later clarified that this was when the core temperature of the body was below thirty degrees, more than seven degrees below the norm. They weren't there yet. The tale-tell signs were if Simon's shivering stopped and he resembled a breathing corpse, then and only then would he have entered this dreaded metabolic icebox.

Dennis also knew from his Antarctica thriller that the body's temperature could be raised by two degrees an hour and this was fundamentally what Grace was hoping to achieve.

Grace was still angry that Jeff and the others hadn't listened to her insistence for them to provide a hat for Simon's shaved head when putting him in the equipment shed, so much vital body heat had been lost because of this.

Tired and guilty, they were all secretly glad that they were no longer required to nurse Simon. It was Grace's responsibility now.

Jeff, the one who had been convincing everyone of Simon's guilt, had locked himself in his room and was not answering to anybody.

They all suspected as they ate, but did not say, that Jeff's solitude was the onset of clinical paranoia.

But the madness was only beginning for the rest of them.

A madness coming from the very idea that a killer was still among them.

"I'm afraid of death... Yes, but that doesn't stop death coming."

Agatha Christie, *And Then There Were None*

PART 4

Secrets and Confessions

Chapter Fifteen

I

After dinner, Patrick suggested that Dennis and Terry join him in a game of poker. They accepted. The simple logic was that if they were all in one place then the killer couldn't commit another murder.

Dennis won the first hand with a solitary king as the high card.

"Your turn to deal, Terry."

"Sure."

As they studied each other with each hand dealt, they couldn't stop thinking that someone's act went way beyond the clichéd poker face. The ex living up to his claim of brilliance, anticipating every guest's mood and reaction before they knew it themselves. Patrick couldn't help but think of the trap he'd walked into.

"Check," Patrick said, looking at Dennis to gauge a reaction and seeing nothing telling in it.

Patrick stopped concentrating on the cards, so he lost again.

"Raise," Patrick said to Dennis.

"I'll see you," Dennis said.

"Thought you might." Terry turned over the fifth community card. It was the nine of spades. It was no good for Patrick but he guessed from Dennis' reaction it was no good for him either. Unless he was bluffing again.

"Re-raise," Patrick replied without hesitation.

"That's the spirit," Dennis said. "I'll see you."

"Take me down then." Patrick smiled. "I fear the nine helped you."

Patrick turned over a pair of sevens. The seven of hearts as the third community card gave him three of a kind.

"It did," Dennis smiled, revealing his cards.

Dennis had a pair of nines to go with the nine of spades that had just been turned over as the fifth and final community card.

"For Christ sake," Terry said, commenting on the fact that Dennis had won yet again.

Terry dealt the cards again, employing the unfussy riffle shuffle method.

"You thought you had me that time, didn't you?" Dennis said smugly, not taking his eyes off Patrick. "Your eyes told me."

"Hey Shakespeare," Terry said. "We don't want to hear it. Just shut up and play."

Dennis didn't look at his cards, keeping his gaze on Terry.

"No one likes a sore loser," Dennis said.

"I haven't lost yet," Terry reminded Dennis, looking down at his six match sticks. Dennis had at least five times that all ready. "My luck will change."

"If you're thinking like that, trust me it won't."

"Just shut up and play," Terry said, unable to resist smiling back at Dennis.

Terry chucked two matchsticks into the middle. The betting remained light for Terry as he set his trap.

"Fold," Dennis said. "I'm folding because Terry finally has his two pair and Patrick his Queens."

"Really?" Terry said. "You honestly think you're that good?" But Patrick could see Terry was annoyed that Dennis had read him blind again. Patrick did have a pair of queens and he'd noticed that Terry subconsciously touched his left earlobe every time he had a decent hand.

As an hour turned into two, and although Patrick won a couple of hands, Dennis was simply too good for both Patrick and Terry, confidently raising when he had to. Dennis' calculating decision-making defied the notion of poker being merely gambling. He seemed to be able to pick up on the intricacies of both opponents' play. The bluffing, the readiness in which they called, the subconscious straying of the hands and the facial twitches all utilised by Dennis' honed predatory instinct. Dennis proved equally adept at disguising his plays, his misdirection born of equal skill.

Terry seemed to be blinking more than usual to Patrick, but Patrick couldn't decipher this as meaning he had a hand or was just thinking about making a bullying play ahead of time.

Patrick folded and nodded to Terry. Now was the time to bring this matter up.

"Somebody mentioned to me that Ronnie's death was a copycat of one of the murders in your book." Patrick eyed Dennis' reaction carefully. This was the one that counted.

Terry couldn't resist jumping in. "Is that true?"

"I'm afraid it is," Dennis admitted with a sigh.

Dennis seemed to be glad to have it off his chest. "Grace told you, didn't she?"

Neither Patrick nor Terry confirmed this with an answer.

"I wrote a novel," Dennis admitted, bowing his head in confession. "It's about a rich psychopath who invites a group of strangers to a party in the Austrian Alps."

"Just like this," Terry said.

"Just like this," Dennis confirmed.

"And you still came here?" Terry asked incredulously.

"Without hesitation," Dennis said. "Anna invited me."

II

"And you expect us to believe that?" Terry said, throwing his hands in the air in a theatrical manner.

"How was I to know?" Dennis almost shouted, his composure at the poker table all but lost. "I mean this guy knew everything. Things only Anna and I could have possibly have known."

"Such as?"

"Plus, I had phone calls from a police profiler," Dennis said. "I had his details checked out and they were legit."

"With enough money, you can buy anyone," Patrick said. "That's what you're suggesting?"

"Tell me you're not buying this bullshit?" Terry said to Patrick as if Dennis were no longer in the room. "He lies for a living."

It had the desired effect of angering Dennis. *This was their best chance of tripping Dennis up*, Patrick thought. *Of finally catching him out in a lie.*

"I was duped," Dennis knocked his drink over as he stood up. "Just like you were."

"And what did this man sound like?" Terry replied, not letting up.

"Now that you mention it, not unlike you."

"You're a fucking liar."

"I'm not the only one who thought you were a cop when you turned up," Dennis said to Terry, as though working for the Police was something shady.

Terry stood up to confront Dennis, ignoring Patrick preaching rationality.

"Calm down," Patrick said to both of them, pouring himself another drink from the whisky decanter. "I believe him. A police profiler phoned me too."

"Still doesn't change the fact that he hasn't stopped lying since he came here." Terry sat down and knocked back the shot of whisky Patrick poured him. "He needs to level with us."

"Tell me this," a still standing Dennis said. "If I'm lying, don't you think I would have come up with something better than this nonsense?"

III

They played on half-heartedly. They were only playing for matchsticks still but the life had gone out of the game. Dennis had compiled a miniature bonfire of matchsticks by the time the living room grandfather clock announced it was 11 pm. Shortly after, they conceded that Dennis was unbeatable tonight. Patrick folded for a final time, stood up and announced that he would go check on Simon's condition.

"So, the game's over?" Dennis said to Patrick as if he were surprised Patrick was giving up.

"That's all I've got, I'm afraid," Patrick said. "Well played."

The 'real poker' game going on beyond this was what counted. A game wagering their lives and not mere matchsticks. The three men measured each other once again with a lingering look before Patrick departed.

Patrick returned after a couple of minutes to break up another argument between Dennis and Terry.

"Well?" Terry asked.

"He's stable," Patrick answered, sitting down.

"Good," Terry said tiredly, rubbing his eyes. "That's good."

The game of poker had ultimately only really served to heighten suspicions and hadn't relaxed them as Patrick had intended.

"If you must know, I've been thinking about each of the crimes. All the murders are in my books," an on-edge Dennis confessed with melodrama, interrupting Patrick and Terry's conversation on Simon's treatment. "From a certain point of view."

IV

Dennis returned to his room, turning the heating up as far as it would go. It was obvious from how they were acting in his company that they knew his secret.

He had almost come clean about it to the others, but a confession at this stage would only make him look even more unbalanced. Unbalanced and guilty.

Dennis didn't intend to sleep tonight.

Or read.

He had to act.

V

Dennis returned to the living room to find Patrick still seated at the table. There were four mobile phones laid out on the table in front of

Patrick. Terry came into the room and slapped down five more devices, one of which was Dennis' iPhone, a phone Dennis' couldn't find in his room moments earlier.

"I can't believe we didn't think of this earlier," Terry said.

"Think of what?" Dennis asked. "We can't get a signal up here. We've already tried that."

Terry looked at Dennis and then Patrick, "yes, but there will be other information, texts and maybe even emails cached on our phones."

Terry smiled with satisfaction, "what's the matter?"

Dennis looked away as Terry picked up Dennis' iPhone and said, "afraid I'll find something you don't want me to?"

VI

Jeff knew he was the outsider now, his survival instinct rebelling against sleep deprivation. His mind wouldn't stop racing ahead in its fantasy world, oblivious to the throbbing headache it caused.

He got up and started circling the room, the movement helping him to think.

The silence downstairs spoke of plotting to him. *Yeah, they're plotting against me, biding their time.*

Jeff rubbed his itchy stubble. He knew they all suspected him now and that put him in danger. He had to make sure he got to them first. Attack was always the best form of defence.

It was in that moment of clarity that Jeff, for the first time, knew exactly what he had to do.

Chapter Sixteen

I

Terry's body was discovered in the early hours by Dennis. His corpse strung up for all to see, as much of a trophy as the waxen statue of Anna.

Terry had a gag in his mouth, his bulging eyes conveying that he had died in agony. In his mid-drift, a samurai sword pinned him to the wainscoting. Dennis recognised the missing sword as the one on display in the study behind a glass cabinet of artefacts Anna had brought back from her trip to Japan. The weapon Jeff had threatened him with.

He spotted a message written in blood next to Terry on the wall.

Who am I?

Dennis' hangover reasserted itself as he bent over and threw up.

II

Grace departed Terry's murder scene with Patrick, parting ways as she walked down the long winding corridor to her corner room. It was still dark outside, daybreak due in the next hour.

She found a note tucked under her door. She picked it up and read it immediately:

You're next bitch!

Grace felt eyes on her as she slipped the note into the pocket of her dressing gown but saw no one.

III

Patrick prepared breakfast with Grace. Simon laid out in the adjoining pantry room, the door ajar so that she could keep an eye on him.

"How's he doing?" Patrick finally asked.

"Some of his co-ordination has returned, but he's still drowsy with slurred speech." The look in Grace's hazel eyes told him she thought about keeping something back before deciding against it.

"He's adamant over something about this ex, but what he says makes little sense. I need to keep a close eye on him over the next few hours."

Patrick nodded, taking all this in.

Visions of Terry's dead face still bullied their conscious thoughts.

They had found the eight ball from the pool table lodged in Terry's throat. It had been forced back into his gullet.

The samurai sword a mere finishing decorative touch after death, Grace surmised from her medical knowledge. *A finishing touch to reduce Terry to a serial killer's trophy.*

Patrick levelled his eyes with Grace's as she buttered toast. "You still think it's Jeff, don't you?"

"I don't know what to think anymore." She turned away, perhaps to hide tears, possibly to hide her fear. After a moment she met Patrick's eyes, her face hardened with resolve. "Yes, I do."

"He's locked himself in his room."

"Keep him there."

IV

Dennis and Patrick threw a bedsheet over Terry when they couldn't budge him from the wainscoting. The handle of the sword poked against the white bed sheet to form a tent.

"Great, now it looks like a ghost with an erection," Dennis joked to Patrick. "Much more dignified."

As usual, only Dennis found his jokes amusing.

The sheet abruptly slipped off of the body and they were all drawn to the Samurai sword in Terry's middle.

"The handle looks expensive," Grace offered.

"Was for Terry," Dennis said.

"Don't joke about something like that," an irritated Grace said.

"Sure," Dennis said, protesting his innocence by spreading his palms. "Nerves, Doc. Just nerves, that's all it is."

"Okay," Grace said. "Well, we need to search the house again. We need to make sure that no other lethal weapons are being stashed away by…our killer."

"Of course."

"What about Simon?" Patrick asked.

"We'll leave him locked in the pantry," Grace said, massaging her scalp. "The whole thing shouldn't take more than half an hour."

"Depends on what we find, Doc," Dennis said.

"What do you mean?"

"Well, old houses like this always have secret passageways, entrances and rooms," Dennis smiled to himself. "You really haven't you read any of my books, have you?"

V

With Jeff missing, they searched his vacant room first, followed by everyone else's, including the deceased.

Dennis announced he was going to shower in the master bathroom down the hallway. The instant they heard running water from the shower, Grace and Patrick sprinted to Dennis' room, frantically searching it again, this time more thoroughly. Dennis had been on edge the whole time they'd been through his possessions. There was also the issue of Dennis being unable to remember the password for the protected documents on his phone which Patrick didn't buy at all.

Patrick leafed through a black leather-bound book rather than checking for concealed weapons with Grace.

"What's that you've got there?" Grace asked.

Patrick ignored Grace's question for a moment, turning a page and then another.

"Dennis," Patrick replied after a time, "is planning a non-fiction piece about the events in this house."

"Dennis doesn't admit to any of the killings, except on the night of Jack's disappearance he claims to have been sleepwalking and doesn't know how he came to have a metal stake soaked in blood in his room when he woke up."

"What?"

Patrick flicked forward three pages, speed reading Dennis' scribbled notes. "He thinks someone's toying with him."

A minute later, Patrick laughed to himself, shutting the book. "He's no better off than we are. He's accused just about everybody, including myself, but his prime suspect was Terry. He also thinks Jeff's being mentally unbalanced makes him unpredictable and dangerous. I think he still wants to win our trust though. We can use that."

The running water stopped in the bathroom. Patrick and Grace sprang into action but were too late. Dennis met them in the corridor as they shut his bedroom door.

Drying his hair with a towel, he said. "Find anything interesting?"

For once Dennis wasn't joking.

Chapter Seventeen

I

"We need to find him before it gets dark," Grace said. "At night he can come at us from anywhere."

"Listen to yourselves," Dennis said, still pissed off about catching them going through his things. "Jeff's a vampire now, is he?"

"Maybe he is," Grace replied. "Or maybe he's just a cold-blooded killer who's gone out of his psycho mind, plenty of those in the real world."

"If you say so, Doc."

Grace's brow furrowed in annoyance, "besides, you told us that Jeff was the one who threatened you with that samurai sword. You think any of us could have got that off of him?"

"What about Simon?" Dennis asked.

"He's safe," Grace replied.

"Safe how? The poor guy can't move."

"He's locked away in a safe room," Grace looked away, as she had a habit of doing when she felt under stress.

"Where's safe in this house? Or am I not getting that information?" Dennis smiled wolfishly, "oh, I see."

"You're not going to treat him, so there's no need for you to know," Grace said.

"You need to win our trust back, that's all," Patrick said. "Nothing personal."

"Whatever," Dennis said to the both of them. "Look, if that's how you feel why don't you go after Jeff without me? That suits me just fine, I'll be barricaded in my room. Out of the way."

"Because we need you," Grace replied, her tone softer and more vulnerable as she put a hand on Dennis' shoulder. "Okay."

"There's three of us and one of him," Patrick said in an attempt to restore confidence in the group.

It didn't work.

"You know," Dennis said. "That's exactly what Terry said yesterday, remember?"

Dennis held up four fingers and took one away to make three. "Except he said there's four of us and only one of him. Now there's only three of us."

Before Patrick could respond, Dennis added, "and you two no longer trust me."

Neither of them corrected him on this fact.

II

There was no doubt in Jeff's mind. How she was thinking had got Grace ahead of the others. It had put her in a position where she could have him killed.

It made sense that the only woman in the house would be calling the shots. Typical of modern society. Manipulating the other men into serving her.

Only I can see her for what she is, Jeff punched the wall in frustration. *Fucking bitch.*

And here he was hiding out in this damned tunnel, breathing hard and afraid of his own fucking shadow. Some plan this was.

He'd even lost his samurai sword last night, dropping it when he thought he'd caught a glimpse of a woman that never was.

Jeff was afraid of his own shadow only because last night a female voice had whispered through the door of the dumbwaiter, he was hiding in. It hadn't sounded like Grace at first.

He'd mistaken it for Anna.

The ghost of Anna had never left his side in these tunnels. But the voice last night came from someone alive. Someone trying to coax him out.

"You'll pay for what you did to Simon, you bastard," the voice whispered. "You'll soon get what you deserve."

It was the voice of a killer after revenge and the threat had chilled him.

Jeff had just enough control over his macho rage not to go out into the corridor where the others would surely have been waiting to spring their trap.

Jeff had resisted the urge to lash out, and this was progress.

With the resulting adrenaline rush, came the clear knowledge that he would have to get to Grace before, one way or another, she got to him.

I just need to find another weapon.

As in football, attack always proved the best form of defence. That was his mantra.

Terry would have agreed with him if he was still alive.

III

Grace hadn't planned on the speed with which Jeff knocked her to the floor with a flying elbow, snatching her knife from her. She hadn't counted on his brute, crazed strength.

None of them had.

Jeff held the kitchen knife to her throat and pressed the axe he held in his other hand into her side. This hostage situation resembled an intimate ballroom dance as Grace settled down into resigned defeat.

Patrick knew now was the time to act, but he found his feet rooted to the floor as though he were already dead himself.

IV

"It's got to be her, don't you see?" Jeff pleaded with Patrick and Dennis.

"The ex is a *man*, Jeff," Patrick replied, surprising himself with the steadiness of his voice.

The knife Jeff had taken from her was at Grace's own throat still, but there was a hint of hesitation in his voice. A hint of sanity. Patrick had to keep him talking.

"I've been thinking these past few hours alone in the dark," Jeff said. "The ex was a man. He's dead and now it's this bitch doing the killing."

Jeff finished talking, searching Patrick's eyes but seeing nothing telling in them.

"Why's that so hard for you to believe?" Jeff continued. "Doesn't make a bit of sense now, does it? Unless..."

"Grace killed Ronnie." Patrick finished the implication, trying it on for size. He shook his head after a few seconds.

"Why though?" Patrick said.

"Because she hates men," Jeff's pleading tone desperate. "Men who took her only love."

Patrick could not see past the spattering of blood smeared on Jeff's neck and face.

Whose blood do you have on your hands, Jeff? Patrick wondered. Patrick was buying time. He didn't agree with Jeff's theory that Grace was behind the killing of Ronnie. Jeff could see this too. Grace was making eyes at Patrick too, willing Patrick to keep him talking.

"No, hear me out. It's her. Has to be."

"What about Terry?" Patrick said. "That had to be the work of the ex."

He'd meant the strength to lift and nail Terry's two-hundred pounds to the wall.

"So, the ex killed Terry, maybe," Jeff said. "Because she ordered him too. Maybe the ex is still alive and working with her."

"So, that makes Dennis the ex?"

"I'm not taking it personally," Dennis said holding up a hand.

Not now, Dennis. Patrick thought. *He only has humour and sarcasm for a defence mechanism. That's not normal.*

Patrick saw that Jeff didn't believe that Dennis was the ex either. It just fitted in with the rest of his theory of suspecting Grace. Grace and Dennis working together. Still, the motivation was left unanswered by Jeff.

"How did you get blood on your face?" Dennis asked Jeff.

"It's a fair question," Patrick said when Jeff shook his head as if to say that he didn't have to answer that.

"I ran into a body in one of the rooms between the tunnels."

"Tunnels?" Patrick said. "What tunnels?"

"There's a whole underground maze down there," Jeff said. "There's a trap door in the cellar, behind a wine rack. Cliché I know, but it's there. It leads to a long tunnel that branches out into three more. From there on I got lost."

"And the body's stashed away down there?" Patrick asked.

"Go see for yourselves," Jeff said. "It's been hidden down there out of the way. Probably for days by the smell of it."

"Jack's corpse?" Dennis said.

Jeff shook his head. "Didn't recognise him. He must have been in the house before we got here."

"You know the more you talk," Dennis said bluntly, "the guiltier you look."

Grace wisely remained silent through this, gulping in a breath or two with the little tight razors of steel biting into her throat like metallic stubble. She felt like she was about to faint, the conversation of her hostage negotiation distant and irrelevant.

Patrick took Jeff's sudden loss for words as an admittance of guilt.

"Look at me now," Patrick said. "Let's have the truth. I can tell you're tired and want this over with. Did you kill Terry last night because you thought he was the ex?"

"Like I said," Jeff shook his head slowly as he spoke, "Terry was dead when I found him, if I had come to you then you would have thought that I'd killed him."

Patrick looked down at the axe pressed into Grace's lower ribcage, drawing fresh blood in droplets.

"I ran because I feared you're all after me," Jeff said. "I still fear that."

Jeff's eyes darted around, concentrating on something Patrick and Dennis couldn't see. "I fear that this is a trap."

"It's no trap, I promise," Patrick saw that Grace was losing consciousness. He had to act fast. "And that's the truth about Terry?"

"The truth."

"Okay, I believe you."

There was hope in Jeff's eyes all of a sudden. "You do?"

"I guess it's time I did something about it then," a feral look overtook Jeff's features as he drew the blade across Grace's throat. It told Patrick everything he needed to know.

V

"Listen to me," Dennis said to Jeff. "Consider this before you do anything rash. Okay? These tunnels run into the mountainside, you say?

Tunnels large enough to get lost in, right? Therefore, there's a good chance the real killer is hiding down there too?"

Patrick backed Dennis up. "He's right. Maybe it's been someone else all along. It stands to reason that if the corpse you found has been left undiscovered all this time, our killer could be lurking in there too."

"She won't think twice about carving you up," Jeff said, having none of it. "How can I get that through to you? It's all just a game to her."

Patrick repeated his request for Jeff to surrender the knife. He did so momentarily, and Grace ran to Patrick. At least that is what she intended as Jeff tripped her up as she took her first strides. She hit the floor hard, face first. As she spat out a mouth full of blood onto the marble flooring, he laughed, tossing the axe lightly from hand to hand with playful intent. He looked like he'd enjoy killing her.

"Stay back now," he warned. "This is not a game to *me*, you understand?" He pulled Grace's hair back. She was too weak to scream. "Not a game."

They backed off

All Dennis could think of was that this had to be the man that had savagely killed Terry last night. The man who they hadn't seen all along.

Only he was wrong.

This was no man any more.

This guy was an animal.

VI

Jeff cut a wide, clumsy arc with the axe that caught only light and then the floor. Too eager in the killing stroke, he went down hard on top of Grace. The axe clattered and skidded out of his grasp.

Then Grace had the knife, grabbing it from where Jeff had tucked it into his belt. A momentary reverse of fortunes, but not for long. It all took place in a split-second of tilting mayhem. Suddenly Jeff flipped her over like a crocodile.

"Get him off me!" Grace screamed.

Jeff twisted his knife in one desperate motion toward her upper body, pressing down his full bodyweight so that its tip would dig deep into her torso.

"Got you now, you bitch!" he grunted.

Certain of the killing stroke of applying downward pressure on her heart with the knife, Jeff didn't know where the spilt axe had gone when he'd dropped it behind him.

Until he felt it lodge against his throat.

"It's over, Jeff," Dennis said.

"Last night, we were hardly human anymore."

Agatha Christie, *And Then There Were None*

PART 5

The Tunnels

Chapter Eighteen

I

HOURS LATER...

He couldn't see. It was dark, pitch black. Dennis was flat on his back as he attempted to reach out. Only he couldn't. The rock confines were pressing on him from all around as if he'd been buried alive.

Dennis' senses awoke, his dry mouth too parched for his cry to carry. "Doc? Patrick?"

These tunnels ran so deep into the mountainside they were insulated from the bitter cold elements outside.

Jeff had been telling the truth about that.

"Doc?" his pleading voice echoed. "Doc, Patrick, are you there?"

Dennis had split from the others when he fell behind and was left with a choice of two corridors. He had chosen the wrong path.

Dennis rubbed a bump on his forehead caused by hitting his head on a low ceiling. It throbbed like hell but was not sticky. His vision seemed okay as he extended the light of his flashlight to reveal yet another dead end.

"Doc! Patrick!" he shouted again, rubbing his head. "Grace!"

He heard the returning echo of his urgent voice and nothing else.

After a time, he found his way into an antechamber where he could stand up again.

A switch activated a string of naked low wattage bulbs hung from a cable and running into each of the tunnels. They hung from wooden and steel supports repeating every five to ten metres depending on the height and length of the tunnel you were in. Not all of the bulbs were illuminated though. Probably less than half lit-up, and many of those were flickering.

Dennis wouldn't walk down the dimly lit tunnel just yet. The backs of his legs were taut and refused to straighten for a moment. His lower back continued to plague him, gripping his neurons with vice-like nausea. His flabby belly had scratches and flaming cuts where he'd crawled over a rough rock in the confined shaft adjoining this one.

His flashlight revealed blood on the floor in front of him, a trail leading into one of the tunnels. A tunnel he could at least stand up in.

Or walk straight into the trap of his foe.

Dennis followed the blood trail until it abruptly stopped, fearing that he'd walked into a trap when he heard a rustling sound.

A rat slithered past him, scratching itself before moving on.

That was the least of Dennis' problems, however, as a silhouetted figure watched him from a distance of no more than ten yards.

Dennis recoiled as he shone his flashlight into the face of Patrick.

"Dennis?"

To Die For

It was Patrick's face but it didn't sound like his voice. He didn't seem surprised to find Dennis.

"Where's Grace?" Dennis said.

Patrick hesitated. "This place is bigger than the house itself!" He panted, out of breath slightly. "A lot bigger."

"That's not what I asked."

Dennis saw for the first time that Patrick's calm demeanour was possibly a front. A front for a completely different personality maybe.

Patrick clutched a gleaming steak knife. A blade Dennis' eyes nor torch beam would leave. There was no blood on the knife, but he could have wiped it clean.

"What have you done with Grace?" Dennis asked in a soft whisper.

"She's just down here," Patrick pointed behind him. "Come see for yourself."

Dennis desperately scanned the rough stone floor.

Tossing his flashlight to Patrick, Dennis bent down and slipped a rock behind his back.

II

They climbed the ladder, Patrick leading the way. He opened a hatch leading to a stone antechamber.

Shards of piercing light shot out their dusty brilliance revealing only more stone walls ahead.

A considerable quantity of food had been stashed away down here. Cereal boxes, tins, as well as rice and nuts in neat plastic containers. Cigarette butts and an Austrian chocolate bar wrapper scrunched under Dennis' boots.

Was this Patrick's hideout he'd happened upon?

"If you're hungry?" a voice startled Dennis. "The good stuff is down here."

It was Grace.

Dennis breathed a sigh of relief.

III

"All of us had the opportunity," Grace said, demolishing a dark chocolate bar. "But Jeff was the only one unaccounted for all evening."

"Of the five of us left," Dennis persisted, "Ronnie's death only clears Simon."

"We need to find the body Jeff said was down here," Patrick interrupted irritably.

"We're where he said it would be," Grace said.

"Maybe he got confused," Dennis replied. "It's easy to get lost down here."

"We won't find it," Grace said.

Dennis exhaled sharply. "And what makes you so sure Jeff did it?"

"I just know."

"How do we know Jeff is the ex and not a guy lashing out because he's scared shitless?" Dennis said. "I mean, I came damned close to braining Patrick just now."

Patrick looked at Dennis with concern.

"No offence," Dennis said.

"I know it's him, okay?" Grace repeated tiredly. "Trust me."

"What about this place?" Patrick said, looking around.

"What about it?" Grace said.

"Samuel Wentworth built it," Dennis said. "He had a crew working up here throughout the fifties and early sixties. Must have feared a nuclear war or something. Who knows how eccentric shipping millionaires think?"

"It could be a drug cartel tunnel," Grace said.

Dennis shook his head, "we're too far from the border for that, Doc."

"Do you think the ex is related to the Wentworths then?" Patrick said.

Dennis shrugged. "I don't see how knowing that's going to help us at this point."

"It's Jeff," Grace said decisively, unable to keep the shortness out of her tone. "It's Jeff and those drugs are going to run out soon." She looked to Patrick. "We need to get moving if we're going to search all of the tunnels."

Grace was referring to the dosage of crushed painkillers she'd mixed into Jeff's dinner to make him docile. The room had been locked and a dresser pulled up against it from the outside, but Jeff was resourceful.

"Okay," Patrick motioned to a tunnel to the left of them. "This way, I guess?"

"You're sure?"

"Well, it's the only route we haven't taken."

They climbed into a crawlspace no bigger than a water-chute slide.

Grace, keen to get back to Simon, was out in front. Patrick in the middle, with Dennis lagging behind.

The rough stone on their elbows was replaced with smoother stone as they got deeper into the tunnel. Dirty carpet mats had been placed further along this tunnel. They hoped this was a sign that they were getting nearer the house. It made sense.

Dennis found the silence coupled with the claustrophobia unbearable. "You think we'll find Jack down here?"

"We have to keep looking," Patrick said.

IV

"Alright," Grace said. "Why were you so keen to get me away from Dennis?"

"He keeps lying to us," Patrick said. "I read some of the emails on his phone, the one's he said he couldn't get into."

"And?"

"Anna didn't invite him here," Patrick whispered, he looked back at the door to check Dennis wasn't eavesdropping. "Quite the opposite, in fact. She explicitly told him not to contact her again. Ever."

Grace put an arm on his shoulder, looking intently in his eyes. "Don't let on that you know that Anna pushed him away," she bit her lip. "I know it's Jeff. Dennis is just worried we suspect him. It's making him behave oddly, that's all."

V

Dennis, cold, sober and all alone, thought about what Patrick had said about the ex. He couldn't stop thinking about it.

"You have to understand that he believes he's God." Patrick had said, his dark eyes full of warning. "Not just thinks it, *believes* it, Dennis. And each killing is confirming that belief."

More like the Devil, Dennis had thought. *The Devil laughing at us with every murder.*

Dennis attempted to make his mind a blank page as he gritted his teeth and removed his thick Billabong snowboarder's jacket in order to fit himself into yet another cramped crawlspace.

It was uncomfortably dark and cold as he slithered forward with his torch wedged in his mouth. Patrick and Grace had wisely taken the tunnel which had led them into the dumbwaiter in the pantry on the ground floor. Dennis ate with them briefly before returning back down the shaft which led to this tunnel. They respected his decision to go back.

As much as Dennis wanted to stay with them, he knew the answers to this mystery lay down one of these tunnels.

We're all behaving like animals now, Dennis thought. *Tired and afraid animals. Except for one of us, the one who's the chameleon and the predator at all times.*

Dennis had advanced no more than twenty feet into the next tunnel before he heard something creeping behind him.

Dennis strained his neck to its limit and shone his torch beam back into the stone antechamber.

Two predatory eyes stared intently back at him.

Chapter Nineteen

I

If Dennis' drunken forays into this mystery proved unenlightening, this was not the case with Patrick's sessions so far with Jeff. Jeff was not what he appeared to be. This was a complex mind at work.

Under these conditions, Jeff was not willing to admit anything.

In the second and longest session, a marathon three-hour excursion into the unhinged mind of Jeff Yates, he admitted that he had once assumed the role of the ex to get back at Anna. Patrick later related all this to Grace as they prepared a meal for five. The meal was not being prepared by Patrick alone as he had sworn to Jeff. What Jeff didn't know wouldn't hurt him.

Patrick felt safer with the drugs making Jeff docile.

Jeff, as it happened, had spied Anna one day on the Fulham Road coming out of a boutique, hand in hand with Dennis. Six months after her disappearance from their whirling romance while holidaying in Italy. A disappearance Jeff had gone to the Rome police with.

Jeff was confused and hurt. Hurt that turned to anger.

Anna was then making her living as a fashion model, renting a high-rise penthouse apartment in Chelsea. Monstrous in its tower block construction, it's packing of as many well-to-do residents into the smallest square footage of economical but luxurious living possible had instantly recalled Anna's taste for high-class urban life.

Jeff followed Anna at a distance, spending every minute of his weekends on business in London in an adjacent hotel room across from her apartment block looking through a high magnification telescope.

Jeff's infatuation with her was getting beyond his control.

He admitted to hating himself during this time and the destructive hold she had over him.

He had distorted his voice with an electronic device sufficiently well to assume the role of the ex in a credible fashion. Anna had previously given him enough background info for him to probe and bully in this manner in the assumed role.

Anna eventually moved out of the high-rise apartment, leaving half her belongings and yet another mystery. The stalking had lasted six months and he felt for the first time since Anna had left him that he had control again. He thought he'd never see her again, and that he'd disrupted her life to compensate for how she had derailed his, and they were even. Jeff took therapy and moved on with his life. The texts and e-mails that started flooding in a month ago opened up feelings he'd repressed so deeply Jeff didn't realise he still had them and he sought out Anna here in Austria like the rest of them.

"You buy it?" Grace stopped emptying a tin of tomato puree onto pasta to study Patrick.

Patrick rubbed his temples. "I believe he was telling me the truth, yes."

"Did he admit to any of the murders here?"

188

"No, I think this is just the first part of his admittance to himself more than to anyone else of how he's spent his life. I feel there's more to come. When he opens up his trust to me."

"Does he have dissociative-split-personality-disorder?"

"Possibly," Patrick thought about this for a second. "But probably not. That's a rare disorder, much rarer than books and movies like to make out."

"You've checked he's still in his room?"

"He only feels safe in there now. Feels we're all against him."

"I don't believe that, not for a second." Grace's face was set, without emotion. "That's what he wants you to think. He's leading you on, hoping to gain your confidence again."

"Possibly, but I don't think so. I need more time with him."

"Here, take this." Grace passed him the steak knife, urging him to conceal it on himself in his further sessions with Jeff.

"I'm okay, thanks."

"You might need it."

"I've already got one."

II

Jeff's corner room, the smallest in the house, was like something out of a Dickens novel. Steeped in darkness, it smelled of mothballs and old books. Isolated in the oldest part of the house, the room was located away from the other rooms on the second floor, accessible only by a long narrow corridor with low oak beam arches.

Against Grace's wishes, Patrick was alone with Jeff in this room. Patrick insisted Jeff did not drink beer during their sessions but Jeff seemed all the more anxious for it.

An uncomfortable silence developed when Jeff stalled on yet another of Patrick's probing questions into Jeff's past relationship with Anna. The wind rattled the glass of the room's only window making it difficult for Patrick to catch every word Jeff spoke.

"Let's discuss what happened yesterday," Patrick said after a long period of reflective silence. "What's the first thing you remember? Take your time now."

Jeff put a hand to his forehead, massaging it. "I don't recall much. Just being held down after I grabbed Grace."

"Okay, that's good. We need to get back to –"

"Let me guess, my childhood?" Jeff interrupted sneering, "Or what about my break up again? Why not go over those old wounds one more time while a fucking murderer plots her next crime?"

Now it was Patrick's turn to massage his forehead as it was hurting him, "we can resume later if you'd rather take a break."

"No," Jeff flew out of his seat, snatching his nearly empty glass of orange juice, pouring the remaining contents onto the floor like a petulant child. "You need to shut up and listen to what I'm saying."

"I'm listening."

"I'll let you into a little secret, and if I do, you'll give me a real drink to help me sleep tonight?"

"I'll see what I can do."

Jeff squeezed the glass in his hand until it broke, pressing the shards into his palm with his fingers. "You think I'm bleeding?" Jeff smiled as he held out his dripping hand. "None of this is real."

Jeff moved towards Patrick before he could respond, "and neither are you mate."

III

Coming up the stairs to check on Patrick, Grace witnessed Jeff holding a shard of glass to Patrick's throat before he slammed the door shut on her. She had arrived a split-second too late.

He'd played them all for fools, Patrick included.

He had his hostage, but with nowhere to go Jeff had nothing to negotiate with beyond instilling further fear into her. Patrick would surely agree.

"Patrick?" Grace shouted.

She didn't get a response when she shouted Patrick's name again.

The oak door had been locked from the inside and so all she could do was wait. Jeff had slyly seized keys to the house and outbuildings early on in his stay and stashed them away, Terry had told them that. A useful advantage in covering his crimes maybe?

It all made sense to Grace now.

"Patrick?"

Grace was wary that she had left Simon all alone and Dennis was nowhere to be seen. She banged on the door again in desperation.

"Answer me."

IV

Jeff was making no demands, and so she feared the worst for Patrick.

Grace took the axe they'd kept in the pantry, the one she'd taken off Jeff, to break down the door. Grace, in her adrenaline rush, felt like taking on Jeff with it herself.

How she longed to bury it into his forehead. Right between his eyes.

"Patrick, can you hear me? Patrick!"

Even with the axe in full swing, the door took an unbearably long time to dismantle into splints and provide a sufficient gap in which to slip her hand through and unlock the door from the inside.

Patrick's fate bullied her thoughts. Surely, he would be lying dead on the ground.

She heard glass smash inside that room, guessing Jeff had escaped out onto the ledge that circumnavigated the second floor. It was icy, but for him to fall to his death was too much to ask.

God certainly hadn't answered any of her prayers so far in this damned house.

She spied Patrick's head lying on the ground, framed angelically in sparkling diamond sized fragments of broken glass. Grace frantically forced her way through the door panel, reaching her hand in to manipulate the inner handle.

To her surprise and relief, Patrick was still breathing when she eventually got to him. Even more surprising was that, other than a nasty bump on his forehead, she couldn't find a mark on him.

"Patrick!"

"Grace?" he said groggily as he came to.

"Stay here until I come back, Simon is all alone. I must go."

Grace ran, axe in hand, down the stairs on her way to Simon.

On the stairs, she heard a tinkling rattle, unmistakably a ground floor window being broken.

The banshee wind masked further noises.

A deranged but resourceful Jeff had been playing for this all along, she now realised. A game to get a helpless Simon on his own.

The only hope she had left was that Jeff, locked in his room for the past twenty-four hours, didn't know exactly where Simon had been moved to. Patrick wouldn't have told him and the pantry wasn't the obvious choice.

She hurried. Praying that the house was too vast for Jeff to locate Simon.

V

The night passed into Christmas Eve, but no one was much in the mood for celebrating or even acknowledging this fact. It was just another day they might not see out. Grace had reached Simon first, but Jeff was still unaccounted for, lurking somewhere in the house.

And she knew Jeff, more than ever, was desperate to kill her.

Patrick had found his way down to Grace and Simon, making up a threesome crammed into the servant's dining area, a pokey pantry adjoining the kitchen and main dining room.

They continually heard distant noises throughout the creaking house.

Jeff on the move? Grace wanted to believe Jeff was upstairs. *Upstairs and not watching and waiting for them in the corridor outside.*

Dennis was still missing. They hadn't seen him since he'd retreated into the tunnels.

Grace hoped that the two of them could successfully overpower Jeff. Even a deranged, knife-wielding Jeff. They all shivered, but only Simon had hypothermia.

Grace was shaking with fear.

VI

Shortly after the grandfather clock in the hall chimed once for 1 am, Jeff gave them all an early Christmas present as he located the generator in a basement room behind the gym and the spa area where Ronnie had had his throat slashed.

The lights around the house dimmed for a second before going out completely.

The third swing of the ancient mountaineering pickaxe he'd found in a store cupboard achieving this feat.

This metal clang was followed by a droning whine indicating that the generator was losing power. The generator looked so old Jeff thought it might have packed up on its own anyway.

"This is going to mess up their little plan," Jeff sniggered crazily to himself. "Fuck them right up."

Jeff celebrated this destruction with another slug of vodka. He hadn't eaten for sixteen hours but the vodka in his belly felt good. It had been good for his nerves too.

Jeff gulped another gasping mouthful of the sweet fiery vodka to celebrate that he now had a fighting chance in the complete obliteration of this generator.

And a fighting chance in this total darkness, being better than anything he'd had so far in this godforsaken place, Jeff would take.

"How're you going to watch me now you calculating bitch?" Jeff grunted as he fumbled his way one-handed up the stairs. In his other hand was the axe, his most precious possession, held close to his body.

Jeff was acutely aware that Grace had an axe too.

Chapter Twenty

I

The power going out had come at the worst time for Grace and Patrick as they attempted to move Simon into a warmer room.

The plan was to move Simon into the nearest bedroom, but his limbs were not responding as Grace had hoped they would and he was getting too heavy to manage with each footstep taken.

"Left here, that's it," Patrick said, grunting with effort. Patrick and Grace were shuffling Simon back into the pantry, each under an arm, evenly supporting his weight.

They were surprised and relieved when they made it back. They could barely see three feet in front of them with all the lights out.

There were candles in the overhead cupboards, and this pantry was cosy and came stocked with food in numerous tins. The reason for selecting this place as their hideout.

Grace lit the Calor gas stove and heated some tinned spaghetti, a can for each of them as she poured on the watery Bolognese sauce. As soon as they settled down to eat it by candlelight, they heard a noise.

"Hear that?" Grace whispered to Patrick

Footsteps.

Patrick bravely opened the pantry door, shining his torch into the hallway.

"Someone's coming," Patrick whispered to Grace.

"Don't be a fool," Grace whispered back to him. "Come back in here."

Patrick shook his head. To Grace's disbelief, he exited into the hallway, "no more running."

Grace, behind him, had her knife poised to strike again and again. Ready to maul Jeff's face and body with the blade until she tasted coppery blood on her lips like some nocturnal beast. She gritted her teeth, ready as she ever would be to do what was necessary to end this nightmare.

"No more running." She repeated Patrick's words to herself in a whispered mantra.

II

Those dark predatory eyes fixed on him had soon been accompanied by a dozen more.

Dennis was facing his greatest fear, crawling towards the rats in the darkness.

The bloody things crawled up and down his hands and legs, but he had to keep moving. He shone his torch in the direction of the rats and predatory eyes became luminous alien beads.

"You want a piece of me?" Dennis shouted. "I bet you do."

The rats were a moving carpet of hair and tails that never stopped breaking into highways of scratching and screeching when he shone his flashlight on them.

"Keep going," Dennis said to himself. "Not much further."

Dennis reasoned that if he followed this mischief of rats, he'd discover the dead body they were surely feasting on. The dead body Jeff had claimed to have discovered must be straight ahead. Dennis also reasoned that if there were vermin there had to be a way back to the house via this tunnel too.

That was the hope he was clinging to.

Dennis felt the skin on the back of his neck crawl, "God no!"

A rat had found its way under his jumper.

He turned over on his back to crush the offending rat, who scarpered away wounded. Laid out on the floor, Dennis came face-to-face with at least six more. Two more climbed on top of him, poised to bite.

"Get off me," he hissed.

Dennis thought he'd been bitten, but recognised it was just the cuts and grazes from crawling on uneven stone. He thought about using his flashlight to beat the little blighters to death, crushing them like cockroaches, but was afraid of what he'd do if the flashlight smashed and left him in total darkness and at the mercy of these vile creatures.

With a very unmanly scream, Dennis pushed through the hairy barrier and stumbled heavily and awkwardly into a large antechamber, putting his back out in the process.

He felt the squelch of a rat on his back as he hit the rough stone floor.

"You're a prat, Dennis Harker," he said to himself, gingerly getting back to his feet. "A five-star prat who reeks of rat shit."

Dennis stopped midsentence, holding his breath. There was something else in this unlit chamber, he could sense it. Eyes were on him. Eyes not of the rodent variety.

Dennis cried out as he shone his torch into the face of another man.

"From a very early age, I knew very strongly the lust to kill."

Agatha Christie, *And Then There Were None*

PART 6

The Last Night Together

Chapter Twenty-One

I

Jeff, axe in hand, knew he had to tread carefully as he was outnumbered. He would plan to pick them off one by one in the darkness before morning came.

II

Dennis shone his torch into the face of another man.

"You nearly killed me," Dennis said, patting his heart.

Dennis examined the corpse's face.

It wasn't Jack, there was enough flesh left on the face to see that.

"Who are you, my friend?" Dennis asked, lighting up a cigarette for his nerves.

Whoever John Doe in the red checked shirt was didn't matter. What mattered was Jeff had been telling the truth about the body. John Doe had been killed by some kind of violent poisoning, the bulbous eyes telling Dennis it had been excruciatingly painful.

"Who's behind all this?" Dennis asked, looking at his reflection in the corpse's eyes.

"Ah the silent type, hey?"

"What's that? Me? Nice of you to ask," Dennis was shocked by his maniacal laughter. "Oh, I'm just a rat in a fucking maze down here."

Dennis stubbed out his cigarette moments after lighting it, swiftly moving down the tunnel he'd come from.

Dennis exited another rat-free tunnel, this one leading to the house.

Only Dennis couldn't find the others in the house.

Whatever had gone down was not good.

The house was in complete darkness. By the time he'd pressed the third light switch without any joy, he concluded that the power was out.

Dennis cautiously made his way out of the hallway and into the lounge, mostly by fumbling touch.

Like the rest of the house, he found it to be silent and empty.

III

"Drop it!" Patrick said, wedging a knife into the man's throat. Patrick's strained voice was unrecognisable to himself. "Slowly, that's it."

A flashlight hit the floor.

"Easy," a familiar voice said. "Don't do anything rash."

Patrick withdrew the knife.

"Who is it?" Grace whispered from behind Patrick.

"It's all right," Patrick reassured her. "It's only Dennis."

"Thank God."

IV

"We can't just sit and wait," Patrick said.

They were huddled in the pantry room, where they'd found a packet of candles in the cupboard. By the time the fourth lit candle was placed on the shelf, the light in the pantry was nothing approaching what its overhead strip lighting would have supplied them with, but far more seasonal.

Feels like we're lighting candles at an altar, Patrick thought, with claustrophobic anxiety. *Lighting candles at an altar ready to pray.*

"Stay," Dennis reasoned with Patrick. "It's our best chance. Think logically. While we're in here, there's only one way Jeff can come for us."

"And we'll be ready for him," Grace said, backing Dennis up.

"Exactly," Dennis said. "So just sit down and make yourself comfortable."

The darkness had stirred their survival instinct but not calmed their nerves.

Simon remained on the floor sleeping, no longer shivering, but not speaking either. The unsaid truth was that he was dying.

Dennis, out of G&T, sipped Merlot and gorged himself on the packet of digestive biscuits he'd found in the cupboard while searching for more candles.

Grace, having finished tending to Patrick's bandaged head, drank her herbal tea occasionally, for the sake of doing something more than anything, her hands shaking each time she raised the cup to her lips.

"You find anything in the tunnels?" Grace asked Dennis.

Dennis thought about telling her the truth, before shaking his head. "No, you were right, there's nothing down there."

"Did you get far into that tunnel we left?"

"I met a few rat friends down there and had to turn back."

"Did you get bitten?"

"Don't think so, Doc."

"Here," Grace said tugging at his jumper. "Let me have a look."

V

Grace finished tending to Dennis' cuts as the grandfather clock chimed 3 am, announcing that they were still hours away from daylight.

They'd hear Jeff's approach the moment he came down that creaking corridor. This made it, in a strategic sense, the best room in the house for them to be in. They were surrounded by the darkest, winding corridors and the noisiest floorboards. Only this did not feel like reassurance. It felt like knowing your death in advance.

The other obvious advantage about hiding out in a pantry was there was plenty of food and drink as a comfort.

It was their only comfort.

Patrick lit a fresh candle, placing a handkerchief around his wrist so that the wax didn't drip onto his hand. "I can't sit around here all night. I'll go see if I can reason with him."

"He'll kill you," Grace said.

"He didn't before."

"I'll go with you then," Grace said.

Patrick shook his head, "no, you two stay with Simon. There's a flashlight in my room. Once I find it, it'll only take a couple of minutes for me to get back here."

Patrick refused Grace's offer of a knife or Dennis thrusting an axe into his hands.

"He'll only take it from me," Patrick said. "If I go unarmed, he might trust me enough to talk some sense into him."

Grace, seeing there was no changing his mind, tucked the knife under Simon's bedding instead.

Grace was left thinking, as Patrick slipped into the darkness, that this was either lunacy or bravery on his part. It seemed a combination of the two.

VI

Grace followed Patrick into the corridor. The only light coming from the candles they held.

"Wait," Grace whispered.

"What is it?" Patrick said.

"Here," Grace said, removing her crucifix necklace. "If you're not going to take a weapon, at least take this."

Patrick took it, "you believe he's the Devil himself?"

She dropped her eyes as she nodded, "I know how it sounds, and from a woman of science."

"He's not the Devil. It's all just a show," Patrick gestured around him. "The lights going out."

"A show?"

"An act so that we don't see him for what he is. Weak, vulnerable, alone."

"Jeff is Jeff, but I believe an evil spirit – the Devil – has taken over his body. Every culture believes in this manifestation of evil. Please just take the bloody knife."

"You wouldn't believe how many times I've come across that theory in psychiatry, Grace. And it's always disproved. Always."

"If you read the Bible this is what the Devil does. It's all he does."

"You're frightened, that's all. It's a normal enough reaction to these unusual circumstances."

"Answer me this," Grace said. "How has he managed to kill everyone in his way so far?"

"How do I go about proving to you that he's just a man?"

"By doing two things," Grace looked past Patrick momentarily. "By finding him." She looked Patrick in the eye. "And killing him."

Chapter Twenty-Two

I

Two hours later…

Grace could hear footsteps approaching as she peered out into the darkness of the hallway.

Grace was all alone in the eerie candlelit pantry. All alone except for a barely responsive Simon.

This wasn't another false alarm, another jumpy moment her senses had conjured. This was it.

Time to prove herself.

II

Grace willed herself to remain calm. As still and silent as she could manage, Grace moved forwards, clutching the knife in her right hand and a candle in her left, readying herself to bury the blade up to the hilt into the flesh of Jeff.

"Patrick?"

"Dennis?"

A flashlight shone directly into her face from the end of the winding corridor. Her eyes ached for a second before her vision cleared.

"Simon, he's coming," she whispered to the bundle of sheets to fool Jeff that Simon had recovered and that she was not all alone to fend for herself.

When she looked around, Patrick almost walked into her, his face drained of all colour and expression as he stepped into the candlelit pantry.

"You're hurt?" Grace said, still in shock.

Patrick shook his head. "I'm not wounded."

"Dennis is still out there!" Grace blurted out. Her desperate voice came out in a rasp. "He couldn't sit and wait any longer. Against my advice, he went after you."

Patrick nodded, looking as though he'd been outside in the cold from his colourless complexion. He looked not far from death himself.

"Dennis didn't get far," Patrick said panting, his expression still fixed and grim. "His body's down the hallway."

Dennis too! It took a moment for Grace to compose herself. "The axe?"

"It's stuck in his head."

She turned away in shock. "Jeff?"

"We met upstairs before I located my flashlight," Patrick said. "I lost him in the darkness."

Grace nodded, taking all this in.

"You had a lucky escape, he must have passed right by you," Patrick said, pointing in the direction of where he'd come from. "As I say, Dennis' body is just down there."

They said nothing more. There was nothing more to say.

They could only wait.

Wait for daybreak.

III

Patrick checked his wristwatch.

7:02am

They'd started to wonder if they'd see daylight again, as they huddled together in that small pantry.

A slither of sunshine peeked over the horizon, dimly illuminating the eastern rooms of the house. Only the statue of Anna and the glass conservatory at the back of the house felt its full glory this early in the day. Anna appearing alive again bathing in the glorious light. Only no one had seen her yet.

Patrick and Grace remained hiding in the pantry, weapons in hand. They waited for Jeff to come.

And waited.

And waited.

IV

Patrick met Grace's studying eyes. They'd not heard so much as a creak of the floorboards in hours. There was daylight to guide them but Grace still felt reluctant to leave a dying Simon to defend himself, refusing to abandon him to pursue Jeff.

Patrick found that admirable.

The pantry felt the size of a telephone box, the walls closing in.

Better to wait for Jeff to come to them. That had been the plan all along. Grace's devised tactic.

Only Jeff wasn't coming for them.

They continued to hear the wind blow and whistle and nothing else.

Chapter Twenty-Three

I

Their voices echoed as if they too were conspiring against them, competing against the blustering wind outside.

"Where is he then?" Grace said, raising her knife. "We've searched all over!"

There was nothing Patrick could say in response. They had searched all three floors of the house, the equipment shed outside and made circling tracks in the surrounding snow.

They concluded their search in the conservatory with Anna looking on dreamily, giving the impression she knew her killer's identity but was giving nothing away.

"What have you done with his body?" Grace said, her voice low as she approached Patrick with her knife.

"I don't understand," Patrick said. "Whose body?"

The knife swished the air between them as Grace showed that she meant business, "no more of your games."

II

"Remember," Patrick found his voice surprisingly steady when he spoke again. He tried not to look down at the kitchen knife inches from his gut, "we've still got to search the tunnels."

Grace shook her head, "you think I'm going down there with you?" She shook her head again. "No way."

"You have to," Patrick said simply, his voice gravelly. Patrick considered giving her a disarming smile and thought better of it. "There's no other way."

The knife trembled in Grace's hand. It trembled from the knowledge that he was right.

She would have to go down into the tunnels with him.

III

The dark cellar felt bitter cold, both of them shaking as if they were in a deep freezer. A tired Grace thought morbidly that this is where they should have put the dead bodies. Patrick slowly descended the steep wooden steps, going first on Grace's instruction. When he made it to the bottom stair, she started her descent. Grace had half expected Patrick to make a run for it into the tunnels.

Daylight slanted in from above, making it possible to see each other without the aid of a flashlight.

He doesn't look like a killer, Grace thought. Doubts were creeping into her exhausted mind. *But, equally, he doesn't seem afraid. Not like I am.*

Grace sensibly stood on the opposite side of the cellar to Patrick. Her eyes unseeing as she ran something over in her mind. She refused to answer any more of his questions. Eventually, she broke the silence.

"Just keep your distance until –"

"Until what, Grace?"

She raised the kitchen knife. "Until I say so, okay?"

"Not a problem."

Jeff was still out there somewhere. That was what Patrick wanted her to believe. She didn't believe it, though. Not anymore.

She could read it on his face, why hadn't she seen it before now?

Patrick is the ex.

"I promise you I'm not going to move from this spot," Patrick said softly, raising his palms in a pushing down motion referring to a calming of Grace's emotions.

"Just put the knife down please, only for a moment."

Grace's face, sweaty with the exhaustion of having stayed up all night, gave nothing away.

"Not a chance. Now tell me again where you were when Ronnie and Terry were killed. You weren't in your room."

"Look at me, Grace. Do you think that I –"

"I stuck up for you with an alibi, remember?" she snapped. "Just as you told me too. Now I want the truth."

"You're just suffering from –"

"Skip that pseudo-Freudian crap for once and tell me where you were exactly for Dennis' murder." She made a point of looking him in the eye.

"You mean Terry's?"

Grace rubbed her left temple with her free hand. She felt faint. She had meant Terry's. She had gone to Patrick's room in the early hours at the time Terry was murdered, only to find him absent. *Why did I say Dennis' murder?* Grace reproached herself. *There's been so many I'm losing track!*

"You're suffering from mental fatigue, Doc," Patrick said softly. "You must be recognising the symptoms yourself."

"Sure Doc," Grace said, sneering sarcastically at the word 'doc'. "But I still need a straight answer from you."

Patrick, his eyes frantically scanning the room for a weapon, continued to go through where he was for the murders. Only what precisely he was doing when Terry was murdered remained a stumbling block for him yet again. A mental block too.

IV

Patrick turned his back on her again to peer into the tunnels, "you must look."

Grace feared this was another one of his games.

"See for yourself," Patrick said. "Please just take a look for me."

Grace nodded. "Okay, but stand over there." She pointed with her knife. "Right up against the wall."

Patrick obligingly moved away from the tunnel entrance into a dark corner, his face eclipsed in shadow as he backed up against the cellar wall.

Grace shone her flashlight down the dark shaft. A shaft leading to a network of further tunnels. The beam caught what Patrick was referring to pretty much right away.

A body lying face down, feet facing her. The body was missing a shoe.

She traced the missing shoe and a thick smeared trail of blood to the opening of the shaft, no more than five feet from where she was standing.

There was far too much blood for the body to be anything other than a corpse.

"Well?" Patrick said.

"Okay, I see it. Who is it though?"

"Looks like Jack to me, but we're going to have to go in to be sure."

Grace nodded. "I'll go then. Don't get any ideas about following me in."

V

Grace squeezed into the shaft, shuffling in back-first, and sliding her way down with her hands. The blood, acting as a lubricant, felt gross on her jeans-clad bottom, and every breath she took smelled of gone-off meat.

She continued sliding down the tunnel in a backwards fashion so that she could have eyes on Patrick the whole time. When she was no more than six or seven yards in, she called him to come forward and shine his torch down the tunnel for her. Grace had her knife ready if he crawled in after her.

Only when Grace was a good ten yards inside the shaft, and closer to the corpse than Patrick shining the torch in her direction, did she twist onto her front in a tight, air-wrenching squeeze and propel herself towards the corpse on her hands and knees.

She had the security of knowing she was considerably faster than Patrick in these tunnels.

"Unless he'd been feigning his slowness earlier," she said to herself. She didn't want to think about that eventuality.

It proved an even tighter squeeze to get up and over the corpse, but she somehow managed it, her back scraping the roof of the tunnel. Grace was too pumped up with adrenaline to acknowledge the bright filaments of pain in her back the friction caused.

She had to get away from Patrick, now more than ever having seen the identity of the corpse.

Grace kept moving in the direction she was going, away from Patrick and away from danger.

She ignored his calling out, "What's going on?"

To her surprise, the frozen terror recorded on the victim's features did not belong to Jack as Patrick had suggested.

VI

"Grace, what's going on?" Patrick said, hearing his voice echo back to him.

Still no answer. Grace had disappeared to the other side of the body and had not reappeared. Patrick, gritting his teeth, climbed in after her. He gripped the rock he'd found in the cellar tightly in his right hand.

VII

It took Patrick less than a minute to reach the dead body. At six-foot-two and two hundred plus pounds, Patrick could not even attempt to squeeze past the corpse. With no room for manoeuvre, he dragged the corpse back up the tunnel where he'd come from.

There was only a slight gradient, but it took Patrick a good fifteen minutes to get the corpse out of the shaft. The whole time he whispered to himself, "makes no sense."

It didn't.

With one last heave, Patrick pulled the body feet first out onto the cellar floor with a slam.

He looked at the corpse's face again in the light of the cellar. The darkness in the tunnel hadn't played tricks on his eyes. There was no mistaking it now.

The face of frozen terror belonged to Jeff.

Chapter Twenty-Four

I

Patrick's flashlight twitch-twitched, threatening to go out any moment now. The tunnel in front of him shaking like an extension of his disturbed mind in the wavering light.

"Grace!" he shouted for what felt like the thousandth time. "Grace?"

The batteries in his flashlight were low and his only thought was of Grace. He had to find her before the damned batteries went dead.

There appeared to be chamber after chamber in this dark womb. A real chamber of horrors.

"Grace, where are you?"

Patrick was hungry and thirsty, his mouth tasting of copper and his empty stomach full of sores.

Patrick heard what sounded like heavy breathing nearby.

"Grace, tell me where you are!" Patrick shouted with renewed hope. "We have to stick together."

The breathing could be heard again, fainter this time. *Was she getting further away?* Patrick wondered. *Can't let her get too far.*

Another person's rustling movement could be heard at the other end of the tunnel, this sound was not a product of his imagination.

Patrick shot into life, forgetting his gashed elbows and knees as he propelled himself forward in a frantic crawl, his hunting knife occasionally scraping against the rough stone floor.

II

It wasn't Grace. It must have been his imagination, after all, Patrick finally decided.

The batteries in his flashlight died, plunging him into darkness. Patrick had treated phobias for years and now he was treating himself.

"Get a grip," Patrick said to himself. "Lose it now and you won't make it out."

Another cold tunnel of darkness greeted him, another rat-infested antechamber and another wrong turn.

"Grace!" he shouted desperately. He wanted to give up and head back to the house but knew he wouldn't.

III

Patrick had crawled back and forth for what seemed like miles. Turn after snaking turn. He had to be outside the walls of the house by now.

Had to be.

Patrick got up off his aching knees to stand.

To Die For

He ascended some steps, lifting a hatch leading to the freezing mountainside.

It was dark outside as a shivering Patrick crept cautiously up to the front of the house, the high-altitude air penetrating his jumper and knifing into his side.

Patrick rubbed his hands and blew warmth into them. He had to get into the house as quickly as possible since he'd removed his parka to fit into the smaller tunnels.

Patrick entered the front porch, keeping down and well out of sight. He felt the warmth of the house soothe his icy face and hands as he tip-toed into the hallway.

Someone is watching me. He could sense it. *Someone watching from up above.*

His fingers tightened around the handle of the knife.

Patrick looked up anxiously.

There was no one there.

IV

Darkness reigned wherever he looked, the only light coming from the moon reflecting on the snow. The wind, indistinguishable from the howls of hungry wolves carrying from far away, added to the eerie atmosphere. Inside the still and silent house, all the framed photographs of Anna were either face down or obscured in spider webs of cracked glass. All the blow-up posters dominating the walls, every last one of them, had been ripped into strips with a knife. Anna's statue remained untouched because it was Anna herself.

V

Grace summoned the guts to enter the room adjoining the pantry to check that Simon wasn't still alive and in pain. She tried to avert her eyes away from Dennis' mutilated corpse as she passed him in the corridor on her way there.

Her heartbeat hammering in her chest the whole time, it took Grace several attempts to pull the sheet back and check Simon wasn't still breathing.

Satisfied Simon was dead, Grace instinctively ran without looking back until she was back in her bedroom.

Simon hadn't faked his illness, the mystery had been solved, but knowing the killer's identity didn't make her feel any less under threat.

An exhausted Grace breathed a sigh of relief that she'd made it back to her bedroom.

She barricaded herself in, locking the door and pulling the dresser up against it as quietly as she could manage.

Her hands were shaking badly with fear as she attempted to calm herself down and prevent the onset of a panic attack.

VI

Grace felt she hadn't the nervous energy left in her body to face off against the ex. She had to rest and hide behind the comfort of a locked bedroom door.

Another train of thought took over her racing mind.

I'm no better off than my first night here, a despairing Grace thought. This is exactly what I'd done then, pulled the dresser across my locked bedroom door for extra security, *and now I'm trapped all over again.*

In truth, she was worse off than her first night here. Her present predicament was a lot worse. But that chain of thought had to go too.

There was only candlelight, and then that was gone too as her only candle burned out altogether and total darkness smothered her. With no heating in the room either, Grace snuggled under the quilt she'd taken from the other bedroom in this corridor.

Grace snuggled under the bed covers and quilt. Fully clothed but still freezing, she wrapped her arms around herself to optimize her body warmth.

Grace's sleep-deprived eyes were about to close and finally rest when she heard a low, devious voice.

The bastard's in the room with me!

It took a few troubled, disorientated seconds of slicing at thin air with her knife to recognise the voice was coming from outside her room.

A bolt of adrenalin surged through Grace's body. Her mobile phone with the dead battery (dead because she'd been using its light to see in the tunnels when her flashlight failed) fell out of her pocket and was lost in the darkness. The phone hit her heel and slid under the bed like an ice hockey puck.

Again, she thought the noise had come from inside the room, as she jumped.

"You're next Grace," the male voice, not sane, sniggered like a child before scratching their fingernails on the bedroom door.

The voice was unrecognisable.

So was her own. "Stay away!"

The scratching abated straight away, and so did the mocking voice.

She'd last slept over twenty-four hours ago and that was only really a nap in the pantry while the others – the ones she had trusted – had been alive to watch over her.

The killer can't get in this room, she told herself. *I must get some rest.*

Grace lay on a cold and hard mattress. The quilt she wrapped around herself in a cocoon of warmth, her only sensual comfort.

Grace gradually felt her racing heartbeat slow and her muscles relax.

She consoled herself with the fact that there was no way into the room for this killer.

But conversely, there was no way out for her now either.

It was a standoff.

"I'll kill you!" the voice whispered seductively through the door, "just like I did all the others."

"No," Grace answered with renewed determination. "I'll kill you."

The maniacal, loony howling greeted her. It took a moment for Grace to recognise this as the killer's high-pitch laughter. The feral scratching of fingernails on wood followed, like a restless animal. These were the last sounds Grace heard before her eyes miraculously closed in sleep.

VII

The patter of heavy rainfall woke Grace. It was the first rain she'd experienced in Austria and the first time in days there'd been no snow falling. She sat up in her bed, looking out of the window in disbelief at the change in weather.

Grace's heartbeat dragged uncomfortably and her breathing became shallow as she remembered where she was. Trapped in this room.

A devious, serial killer waiting outside her door.

And I'm the only one left to fight him!

The dresser was still in its place, she saw, pressed up against the door. She breathed a sigh of relief at that.

She looked unseeingly out of the bedroom window into the dark but dawning day.

Grace opened the window pane and gingerly climbed out onto the ledge that circumnavigated this floor.

The gentle night wind, possibly the only thing gentle in touch in this world now, billowed her jeans, moulding the denim fabric to her leg like pleasantly drying plaster. Her gently shuffling feet made Grace feel cast as the escaped mental patient more than anything else. That and the fact that she was standing on a one-and-a-half-foot ledge fifty feet up.

This was not suicide.

Grace wanted to escape while she was still covered by darkness. There could only be minutes of it left.

From up here, Grace could make out Anna's statue in the middle of the glass conservatory room.

That spooked her all over again, providing Grace with a jolt of nauseating fear she didn't need on this precarious ledge.

She made out a figure moving below.

A silhouetted figure, looking up at her. Grace thought she was dreaming for a moment.

Dreaming a freaky nightmare.

The freakiest of nightmares.

She glanced down out of the corner of her eye. It looked as though he was waiting for her to fall.

After a few seconds, Grace forced herself to look down at him.

His cold eyes moved up to her.

Grace recognised that he was wearing a mask. A fancy-dress accessory depicting a gothic demon with a hooked nose. This was the first detail she noticed about him. The second was that his jumper and jeans were soaked in blood.

The masked figure abruptly shot into life, bounding through the snow at speed, making it clear to Grace that the blood on his clothes was a victim's and not his own.

In the other hand of the masked figure, an object caught the rain and glistened.

The shiny, gleaming steel of a kitchen knife.

VIII

Grace climbed back off the ledge and lowered herself back inside the house through the window.

Grace had to admit to herself that she didn't have the skill to use the ledge as an escape route without risking falling to her death.

She crouched in a squatting position, preparing herself to move the dresser away from the door, knowing that if she acted now, she could get out of this room before the masked figure climbed the stairs to get to her.

She wouldn't be trapped anymore.

Grace hesitated, moving away from the dresser. She knew she couldn't leave.

Not yet.

She climbed back under the sheets. She'd rest some more.

The truth was that she'd become paralysed with fear.

The mask was a powerful symbol of this man's mutilated mayhem. When she faced him, Grace preferred it to be in broad daylight.

Grace hated herself at first for not leaving the bedroom, but as fatigue hit her again, the self-rebuke left her.

She'd made the right choice. This psycho had tried to lure her out of the room with the trap of appearing outside. Psyching her out of her position of safety in the locked bedroom.

This serial killer, a killer Grace started to doubt as being Patrick, was smart at these games.

Grace knew that if she was to survive for much longer, she'd have to be smarter still.

Chapter Twenty-Five

I'm going to starve to death if I don't do anything.

Hungry and thirsty, and left with no other option, Grace pushed the dresser away from the door and left the sanctity of the bedroom.

It felt like a mistake to do so.

She peeked out onto the landing.

Looking right and then left.

And…

No one there.

She felt like running, but walked briskly instead at first, making her way to the pantry. The floorboards creaked in protest enough for her to wince.

She had the knife raised and ready to strike, as she cautiously descended the winding staircase leading to the pantry.

The masked figure had been taunting her at the window again last night.

He'd adopted another tactic to scare the wits out of her.

In his outstretched hand, he'd held a spherical object by strings.

A severed head, held by the locks of its hair.

A head belonging to Dennis it looked like, though she could not be sure.

The thought of this grisly vision from last night forced Grace into a run, the vile imagery bullying her conscious thoughts until she reached the pantry.

The pantry stank of rotten meat where the scent of Dennis' corpse wafted in from the corridor, mixing in with the stench of Simon's equally pungent carcass.

Grace removed her sweater, sweeping up half a dozen cans of tinned fruit, spaghetti and soup into the sweater, turning it into a makeshift carrier bag.

She knew she had to leave this pantry, but couldn't resist running the tap. The water in her cupped hands tasted refreshing and delicious.

Grace, putting her lips to the running water, missed the figure creeping up behind her. She became aware of the intruder only when the pantry door slammed shut.

Grace stopped drinking and snatched up her knife, poised to strike.

Her masked assailant easily batted the blade away, as she watched the knife fly out of her hand.

She felt slow and weak against this maniac.

Grace's last thought was that the masked figure had Jeff's coat on, as well as his jeans and boots. The eyes should have been the only human feature alive in that mask. But these eyes were cold in their immobility.

Just as I thought, it was Jeff all along, Grace reasoned.

Why hadn't the others believed her? These were Jeff's eyes peering from behind the mask and not Patrick's. Jeff had faked his death in the tunnel, she should have examined the body more carefully.

He must have smeared somebody else's blood all over himself and lay down in the tunnels. It was too damned dark to make out anything beyond his identity.

Either that or he was superhuman.

"Jeff no," Grace shouted out, raising her hands in a futile attempt to ward him off. Her last act of defiance against her assailant an ineffective one.

She was losing consciousness.

And blood.

A lot of it.

And then the pain was leaving her body. She felt cold, much colder.

She couldn't even summon the strength to pull the mask from her attacker's face for confirmation of her suspicions.

In the end, she found she didn't care.

For Grace, the ordeal was finally over. She almost welcomed the dark embrace of death when it came.

To Die For

"Death is for other people."

Agatha Christie, *And Then There Were None*

PART 7

Unmasking The Ex

CHAPTER TWENTY-SIX

A FORENSIC FEAST

Ten days later

In my entire career as a SOCO for the Met Police, I must admit I have never seen the likes of this. This bloodbath that has dominated world news since breaking last Friday is making us work overtime. There's more evidence to collate in this crime scene than the rest of the crime scenes I have investigated put together. A slight exaggeration, but that's how it feels.

The icy temperatures have meant that much of the evidence has been left intact, the old house like one big deep freezer preserving everything neatly in stasis.

There are different challenges for us out here.

I'm used to having officers set up a cordon when I arrive to keep back nosey members of the public and overeager reporters from contaminating our crime scene. No such worries here with this isolated retreat necessitating being flown in by helicopter.

In some ways, forensically we are in virgin territory, as I, nor anyone else on my team, has encountered the likes of this in terms of scale or body count.

If I backtrack slightly, we were officially called in after the Austrian police confirmed all the guests as British. That part, at least, was straightforward. All their passports and phones were neatly laid out on a table in the living room.

It is believed that at some point during their Christmas stay, the guests concluded that one of them was a killer and so it was necessary for everyone to produce their passport as proof that they were who they claimed to be.

The Austrian police established that the passports were genuine through cross-referencing the names and dates of birth with the Schengen database to see if any of the guests were wanted criminals.

With their searches not producing a single Schengen alert regarding criminality, they contacted us to aid their enquiries.

All nine guests were found dead along with Anna and her husband, making eleven bodies in all.

We have a detailed timeline of events thanks to Dennis Harker, being a writer by trade, he laid out over a hundred pages of notes on his Samsung tablet. It has proved a useful source in ascertaining what exactly transpired at the Wentworth mansion over the Christmas holidays.

He points the finger at one person alone, Jeff Yates.

I can rule out Jeff Yates though.

Jeff Yates died in the cellar. The same axe that butchered three other people, the murder weapon that seems to have nearly everyone's prints on. He'd been dragged into the tunnels and back out, for what reason I have no idea.

I met Dennis Harker when he did some research for a novel a couple of years back. He shadowed me while I trained some new SOCO recruits back in our learning and development department at HQ.

I have to say, I liked the fella. He was respectful and humble most of the time to me, appreciating that we were accommodating him. Although his jokes were a little distasteful and rubbed some of my colleagues the wrong way, there was something decent about him. I know that's an old-fashioned way to put it but he liked police officers and reflected our profession in a positive light in his resulting book. Trust me, that goes a long way.

I recognised Dennis straight away, he hadn't changed much. Other than his head being split in half by an axe, of course. His scalp has been butchered so badly it reminds me a little of that movie scene with Robert Patrick as the T1000 at the end of Terminator 2, when a shotgun is fired into his head at point-blank range.

Unfortunately for Dennis, he was made of mere flesh and blood and not liquid metal.

The atmosphere of the sprawling house is unsettling to me, but perhaps that maybe because it's the first time I've examined a body I knew in life. But that will not deter me, I feel highly motivated in finding out who did this to Dennis.

When we (eventually) retrieved the data on Grace's phone, we found an unsent text pointing the finger at another suspect.

The text read:

If you're reading this then I have been killed by Patrick Henderson, the madman who invited us here under false pretences and murdered us all.

We found Patrick Henderson halfway down a ravine on the north-west cliff, having fallen almost five hundred metres.

We pulled another body out of a beat-up cable car not far from there, the deceased's face had been banged up so severely that even his dental records couldn't ID him. Only thanks to Dennis' record of events could we confirm his identity as Tony Banks. A third body has been recovered in that same ravine, less than an hour ago, a fallen climber from the gear he had on. IDed as Jack Walterman, a personal trainer from Croydon.

Jack's last goodbye, his final statement to the world, came in the form of a shirtless Instagram selfie from the gym of an Innsbruck budget hotel. It was posted the day before he came here.

There's another lead in the form of a money trail from Sam Wentworth Junior. He hired somebody at a substantial daily rate. We think this person was hired as either a private investigator or as a bodyguard for his wife Anna.

Wentworth was poisoned, his face grotesquely mutilated in the process, but still identifiable. We found him in one of the rat-infested tunnels.

We assumed Anna invited everyone here. That line of inquiry has led to the discovery that Anna had several online identities which make for very interesting reading.

The only meaningful action I've done this evening is to link the victims together on our crime recording system so that it can be put into a single case file if it ever goes to court.

We initially narrowed the killer down to four suspects, and only because Dennis stated that only four other people were alive in his last entry: Simon, Grace, Patrick and Jeff.

There's no earthly way that Grace could have mutilated herself like that, nor Jeff.

That leaves Simon and Patrick.

Simon died of hypothermia and therefore is our chief suspect, coupled with the fact that he's our suspect for the Noel Coward theatre poisoning (another investigation I've still to link on our crime recording system!).

Patrick could have fallen over the cliff's edge after he had disposed of the others. But if we're going down that route then we must also include Jack, who could have hidden away (Dennis mentions him as missing since the second night), before picking his unsuspecting victims off one by one, and later had an accident during his descent.

Now you get an idea of how tricky this job is, and how complex an investigation this has become? Try telling that to the Chief Superintendent.

What at first felt like a holiday – and a unique career opportunity – is starting to get to me, I'll be the first to admit.

Plus, there's the fact that I can't get a signal for love nor money up here to speak to my wife to keep me centred.

I hope that my stay up here is not going to be for much longer. I'm frequently reminded that this has been an expensive favour on the part of the Met Police and a burden on the English taxpayer, and can't go on much longer without a positive result.

We found a mask a few minutes ago, and have lifted a set of prints off of it.

Hopefully, this will lead us to the identity of the killer.

I need a break in this case and I need it soon.

My professional future depends on it.

THE KILLER'S NARRATIVE

(Saved to the hard-drive of a laptop concealed in the clay base of the statue of Anna)

The first murder proved the hardest. I had to ensure that no one saw me leave the terrace steps down to the cable car. Being covered by darkness aided my mission in one sense, but hindered me in another as my progress was slow.

Vandalising the load-bearing metal pulley proved no easy task. Lucklly, I was far enough away that they couldn't hear the racket I was making. The wrench took an unbelievable amount of strength to break the last of the supporting coils and pulleys, pulleys strong enough to support a metric tonne.

I had been gone an hour and so had to make a show of my reappearance, becoming the life of the party, talking to everyone, and suggesting we all play a game of likes and dislikes to get better acquainted with one another.

I started to relax, knowing their only escape route was blocked off, affording me all the time in the world to play my part as a hapless wronged guest and plan the next murder.

That it was Tony who met his demise at the hands of the booby-trapped cable car neither pleased nor displeased me. It could, of course, have been any one of them.

I was planning to strike again, during the early hours of the morning. I was debating who to target next when Jack took the decision out of my hands. I saw the climbing gear catch his eye when I'd accompanied him to the equipment shed. For Jack, this was his ticket out of here. Not trusting anyone, I knew he'd try it alone. I've always been able to get by on four hours of sleep, so I was ready and waiting when he crept past my door. I followed him as closely as I dared. When he took a route down the north-eastern cliff, not an easy descent – and it's not certain that he wouldn't have fallen to his death anyway – I stalked him from the cliffs above. I retreated into the tunnels and was almost face-to-face with him when I removed the clips on the belays and released the rope.

I laughed as he struggled to hang on, it was a nervous reaction that he no doubt mistook for cruelty.

Gravity assisting me once more as it had with the first murder. I rather like killing in this fashion, it seems more natural. Almost regal in its effortlessness.

I'll admit that I took some degree of satisfaction in murdering him. Jack, like the others to follow, reminded me how pathetic I am in my enslaved devotion to Anna.

I made my first telling mistake with Ronnie. Alone with him in Jack's room, my face gave away that I wanted to murder him. I would have killed him then and there had I been certain of the movements of the rest of the house. I couldn't take the risk of making myself the prime suspect. I only made this crucial decision to put the knife down at the last moment when we heard the rest of the group struggle below us. If this had been a fraction later, I would have killed Ronnie, and ended my game prematurely, as it turned out everyone else was present at the fracas ensuing below.

I knew that Ronnie's mind was working overtime with me as his chief suspect and I had to kill him as soon as possible. I slipped some of the poison into the top tea bag in the jar. A slave to routine like the rest of us, he swallowed the poison in his tea.

I followed him to the gym, pretending to work out as I kept an eye on him in the Jacuzzi. He stared back at me the whole time. His eyelids began to get heavier and he started to yell with pain. The less concentrated dosage had started to take effect. He got as far as climbing out of the Jacuzzi before I grabbed him and dragged him under the water, pushing his head down to drown out his cries. Conveniently, he had a dumbbell concealed under his towel for protection which he reached for but couldn't grab in his growing weakness.

I bludgeoned him over the head with it, and that was that. The water meant that I didn't incriminate myself with the fine mist of blood which came from the blow to his head.

I retreated to my room, dried my clothes, and immediately started planning my next murder.

The fact that Jeff now suspected Grace, and vice-versa, developed into a power struggle. I hadn't anticipated this outcome, but I played this rivalry off to its maximum effect thereafter. To keep Jeff and Grace alive as long as possible made sense.

Simon was virtually dead when we retrieved him from the equipment shed the following day, leaving me with one less keen mind to contend with.

Terry, separated from Jeff for the first time, was the next logical target. He couldn't stop his eyes from meeting mine every few seconds.

His bluff in publicly suspecting Dennis was as easy to read as his poker face.

Terry was the hardest to kill in person. God, he nearly ended my mission there and then. He didn't take the poison, which was now in very limited supply anyway after I'd used it on Anna's husband and Ronnie.

Terry was as strong as an ox and highly trained in hand-to-hand combat. Trained to kill. It was sheer desperation – and a lot of luck – that I managed to fall on top of him, the blade plunging deep into his gut. Even then I almost passed out, his legs wrapped around my neck, crushing the breath out of me.

After I knifed him again, I grabbed the samurai sword I'd taken from a sleeping Jeff and thrust it through him, afraid that he'd get up and fight all over again.

Taking place at 4:30 in the morning, no one discovered us. They were all in their rooms behind locked doors. I'm sure I could have made something up if I wanted to, I was that confident at this point. Perhaps overconfident.

I nailed Terry to the wall with the samurai sword, serving as a statement to scare the remaining victims even more. Jeff told Dennis, in true Jeff fashion, that he'd "shut him up and string him up" for betraying him. This, along with the eight-ball I lodged into Terry's throat, made Grace and everyone else firmly suspect Jeff.

It was also taken from one of Dennis' poorer thrillers, but unfortunately, I fathomed that only Tony and myself knew that, and poor old Tony was long gone.

The suspicion of Jeff freed me up to work up a useful relationship with the others.

Jeff nearly killed Grace for me, but his paranoia and general look of guilt made everyone turn on him. He even wrote a note to Grace, saying "you're next", implying he had committed the other murders. By this time everyone was too scared to think rationally about who was where at the time of the murders, as I knew they would be.

Jeff killing the lights by destroying the generator made it that much more exciting for me, and a little easier, I must admit. The survivors jumping at the slightest noise by now, starting to fear this killer as though he were the bogeyman.

Dennis obediently followed me to find Jeff. He handed me the axe in good faith if you can believe it? What a doting fool. A creak at the end of the corridor was enough to make him peer down the corridor. Completely still, he provided me with the perfect target. Dennis didn't even see the axe as I raised it above my head and tightened my core to send it down in a smooth arc and split his head open. I followed it with a second crushing blow which sent his crumpled body down into a seated position.

Jeff, I found in the corridor a short time afterwards. I used the blood on me to the full effect, telling him that Grace had knifed me and I'd knocked her out cold in the cellar. Jeff, predictably headed straight for the cellar. Being pitch black, he paused at the top of the cellar steps and I gave him a firm push. He landed heavily on the stone cellar floor, making a flesh swastika with his legs broken, but was still alive. I used the axe in the same fashion on Jeff as I'd practised with the coup de grace for Dennis.

I dragged Jeff's corpse as far into the cellar tunnel as I could manage, hiding him away. My next victim would have to peer into that cellar tunnel to make out the body, which would provide me with another tactical strike.

With Grace unable to leave the pantry with Simon's condition worsening, I had all time I wanted to play my little cat and mouse game.

Unfortunately, Grace was smarter than I expected. I think the amount of time I'd been gone, particularly the change of clothes into a lighter brown jumper and the duration it took to scrub off the blood on my face in the darkness, using only my mobile phone as a light, the deciding factor in her suspecting me.

That and the fact that we didn't find Jeff anywhere in the house when daylight came.

I intended to kill her in the cellar, but the slippery bitch got away from me.

I don't think I wanted it to end at this point, with all the exhilarating fun I was having. Simon, hardly breathing hours earlier, and without Grace's care, had died of hypothermia by the time I got to him. A very unsatisfactory end for a potentially worthy adversary, and even in his weakened state, I wanted to be the one to administer the killing stroke.

With just Grace and myself playing the game now, I was in the mood for drawing it out.

I found that I liked stalking her. I dressed in Jeff's favourite shirt jumper and trousers, a surprisingly close fit, and donned Anna's husband's masquerade ball mask as the finishing touch. The perfect attire with which to hunt Anna.

My throat was so dry at this point, my sexual excitement growing with the anticipation of the kill, that I even sounded like Jeff as I taunted her.

When I finally cornered her, she cried out "Jeff no!" and I had that feeling of satisfaction that I'd been cheated out of with Simon's death by natural causes in the form of a satisfying final kill.

Perhaps my finest hour, manipulating the side of Grace that despised Jeff at the end.

You see, under duress, we never suspect people through evidence and clear analytical thinking. We suspect people we don't like and we trust people who are socially similar to ourselves. Professionally it's known as unconscious bias. It's what made all of this possible.

Why did I do it?

Well, the first erroneous assumption everybody made was in the primary motivation of the so-called ex. The ex was thought to be consumed by jealousy and wanted revenge. A controlling personality who desired all of Anna's ex-lovers to be expunged from her past, and to completely rewrite Anna's history. A sick mind playing a toxic game with people's lives.

No wonder they couldn't find this man – he never existed!

The true reason for this gathering in the Austrian Alps was far simpler and more human.

Consider this, if you ran over an animal and found it lying in the road barely breathing and in pain, you'd kill right? Put it out of its misery?

This was no different.

The police will say that I took lives, but if these 'victims' had a life for me to take they wouldn't have all turned up the moment Anna clicked her fingers. Wounded, unloved, barely alive, addicted to substances. Every single one of them left suffering from regret by Anna. I simply put them out of their misery.

I did get a sadistic satisfaction from killing them all, I must admit. A vengeful part of me yearned to wipe out every trace of her damned existence. To cut Anna down to something to be worshipped, knowing full well she would have hated to be objectified like that.

Being in that statue was a perfect metaphor for the confined box she had buried me alive in.

I was so close to achieving my perfect life when we got pregnant. When she had the abortion weeks later, I didn't know how to handle it. All she kept saying was how young we were.

I was pathetic when she refused me, but I kept desperately pursuing her as the acceptance of me not being loved by Anna, desired by her, was worse. The idea that I had someone like this in my life, however briefly, and had lost their affection made me loathe myself. I was not enough.

I needed the alter-ego of the ex, at this point, for survival.

As for my suffering, after Anna left me at twenty-one years of age, I was suicidal. I did nothing for a year but hold on. Each night my wrists would throb and I longed to get it over with. I knew that there was not another Anna out there in the world for me. I had no future to look forward to.

After University, I devoted my professional life to discovering how I could get over her. It made sense that my career should be focused around that end, seeing it was all I could think about.

As a practising clinical psychiatrist, I see broken relationships every day of the week. I thought I could be cured, my profession naturally seeking out the cure, but patient after patient confirmed what I'd feared. There was no getting over Anna for me.

She was my soulmate, and whether young or old, rich or poor, famous or infamous, all the accounts about 'the one' amounted to the same thing. There was no getting over the love of your life. It stayed with you like a bad smell. You just got better at coping with it.

So, there was no cure, only coping and compromise. Surviving. Trust me, that is no way to live a life.

In hopeless depression, I started to look to my alter-ego, the ex, for a solution again.

I started to view Anna differently too, like the carrier of a virus who could only cause misery on a massive scale. A virus attacking the human condition rather than the body.

I told myself that the ex was a necessary creation to frighten Anna's suitors away, to prevent her from ruining their lives as she'd obliterated my existence. Only it didn't work.

I knew then that Anna had to die.

These people had taken Anna from me and so had to die too.

I appreciated these exes of Anna were as trapped as myself. Like a stuck record, a cliché of a love song, they couldn't get over her either.

I was reduced to a shell of a man without Anna, and when I saw each of them with her, another part of me died inside, the parts which made me human. I started to feel a growing compulsion to act on the very worst of my desires.

As soon as I committed a murder, I automatically fell back into the guise of the very sane and empathic role of the sober psychiatrist. This happened on every occasion. I think my mind needed it as a coping mechanism. I didn't feel any guilt or remorse after the crime, it wasn't that at all, but more of an immediate reflex to protect my threatened persona and reputation at all costs – one I'd taken years to build up. This innate emotion reverted me to the polar opposite in the duality of my nature. I lashed out with brutal violence only to become the clinical psychiatrist once I'd had my murderous release. It's what averted suspicion away from me so effectively.

People may say I'm crazy for what I did here, but I'd point out that monthly outbreaks of a desperate loner gunning down random victims with an automatic weapon are lunacy. This act had calculation and true meaning, and therefore, has to be considered, without question, to be a sane act.

The guests turning up to Anna's gathering in another country, no matter the stakes, eloquently proves this underlying fact about human nature and its preoccupation with love at all costs. Establishing my theory with the precision of a mathematical formula.

George Orwell wrote that it is more important to be understood than loved, which is why I have detailed everything in my full confession.

The monster of the ex kept growing inside me, there was no off switch for this dark creature. He stalked me as much as he did Anna.

I see now that the ex had this end planned all along. I had created him to keep me alive, to give me power and purpose.

Since there was no one left to ravage and he couldn't live as a real person after this, nor would I be allowed to go on.

I knew months ago that it was all to come to a fitting end at this beautiful retreat. An almost apocalyptic end whereby all of her exes would exist in the microcosm of Anna's final resting place.

To quote another love cliché, I finally proved that Anna was, in every sense of the word 'to die for'.

In all our cases, without exception, this has been proven to be the truth.

Patrick Henderson

THE END

To Die For

An afterthought from the Author

As you've reached the end of my novel, hopefully, that means you enjoyed it. It would mean a great deal to me if you would consider leaving a review on Amazon or Goodreads, or any other site of this nature.

Regardless, I would like to thank you for taking the time to read it.

If you enjoyed it, and are after another book with the same tropes as And Then There Were None, I have also written a novel called The Show, which is also part of my And Then There Were More series.

I'm in the process of writing a third novel in the series, you can find out more about this project if you wish on my website andthenthereweremore.co.uk.

N G Sanders

Printed in Great Britain
by Amazon